MOLLY

What is it About?

ENJOY THE STORY
& STAY GROOVY
GIRL

Owen Crawford

Owen

Published by Poetic Irony Publishing, April, 2021
ISBN: 978-1-8383603-9-9

Editor: Trevor McMonagle - The Right Words Editing
Typeset: Greg Salisbury
Book Cover Design: Lauren Merrett

The author has endeavoured to secure permission from the copyright holders of all quoted material. Any oversight is totally unintentional and the author would be grateful for any errors or omissions to be notified so that corrections can be incorporated in future editions of this book.

All internet addresses given in this book were correct at the time of going to press. The author and publisher regret any inconvenience caused if these details have changed.

The Wanderers & The Lost
May you find your way onto The Path that you never
tire to walk

Acknowledgements

The Family - Your never-ending support for each journey I dare to take.

The Sculptor - Trevor, for sharing your honesty, knowledge, and skill to chisel and refine. You put The Right Words, in The Right Place, at The Right Time.

The Quiche Lorraine - Lauren, the bundle of joy even in dark times. Thank you for designing the perfect cover.

The Dannii - She needs no title. There from the first poem, your opinion I hold dearest. Thank you for everything, always.

The Big Brother - Dools and your infectious laugh. Thank you for the escape to Dublin during the summer of the pandemic, and allowing that final spark of inspiration to finish the story.

The First - Livvie, the first person to read the original manuscript. You brought back my passion to tell this story to a wider audience.

The Green Light - Megan and everyone from The Self Publishing Agency course in October 2020. Strangers with different stories and cultures who found solidarity, support, and similarity.

The Tribe - You bunch of weirdos, the reason I can be comfortable in who I am because of the company I keep. Spread all across this Earth, you are my true definition of family. My view on this world is kept refreshed and my mind culturally updated in each happening of every land. Thanks to you all. May we keep expanding and supporting each other.

The Blow-Up - Each person who has ever offered me a meal and a place to lay my head whenever I find myself wandering or lost. I would never had adventured or grown without your kindness.

The Outsider

A beautiful spring day, the first of many after a long, wet winter. Our Outsider stood alone on The Basketball Court — Blink-182 playing through headphones, cool breeze contrasting with warm spring sun. News of their arrival in The Kingdom had spread fast.

You see, Our Outsider wasn't from a place near these parts, so their accent was the first thing people noticed. The Outsider was new and alone, looking for a fresh start. They had travelled from place to place searching for a spot to call home, each time only to be treated as, well, an outsider, and forced to move on.

And so, this court is the place I would like to start for one main reason.

This Story is My Story.

As the breeze brushed past, The Outsider stepped off The Basketball Court and returned to their car. It was parked the next road over in front of a small studio apartment above a family-run cafe.

They had parked earlier, and, instead of heading inside, had put their headphones on and gone for a walk.

This is such a beautiful spot, The Outsider thought, as they took the headphones off and peered back at The Basketball Court. *I'll have to come back tomorrow and properly enjoy the sunset.*

The Owner of The Cafe was locking up. They both made eye contact, so The Outsider gave him a half-smile and downward nod as a friendly acknowledgement. The Owner smiled in return. "You must be our new neighbour?"

"I am indeed," The Outsider replied.

"I saw your car in the space and was hoping to get the chance to meet you and say hello before the day was out. It's a beautiful town, but I'm biased. I've called it home for thirty-six years."

"It certainly is. So I figured I'd dive in and see what I could make of it."

"That's brave! I'm too much of an over-thinker to ever dare to do that. I worry about every possible detail."

"Well, my life is pretty empty right now," The Outsider chuckled. "Nothing to lose, something to gain."

"Good for you! I'd love to stay and chat a bit more but I've got to get home to my wife and daughter. But if you want, pop down in the morning and have yourself a welcome breakfast, on us. Doubt you've had much time to do a food shop?"

The Outsider showed The Owner their empty open palm. "I have nothing at all."

"Then you don't need a hand carrying anything upstairs."

The Outsider smiled. "There is nothing in the car besides some tools, a pack of gum, and some paperwork."

"Not even a box of clothes?"

"Nothing to lose, something to gain."

The Owner gazed unsure, so Our Outsider gave a reassuring statement.

"It's a fresh start completely for me. I left everything behind and I'm looking to rebuild from scratch. Like that old phrase says, 'Just the clothes on my back and money in my pocket.'"

"Well, you are a very interesting person, aren't you? I'm excited to get to know you, so please do come down tomorrow morning." The Owner's phone started to ring. "The wife. Enjoy your evening, and I'll see you in the morning?"

"That you will. Thank you very much for the invitation, I appreciate it a lot."

The Outsider headed upstairs and unlocked the door to the studio apartment with a sofa, the kitchen sink, and cupboards. The Outsider took off their coat, rolled it into a ball for a pillow, and fell asleep fully clothed on the sofa.

With no blinds and an easterly facing window, the bright beams of sun stretching over the horizon woke them early. The Outsider unrolled the coat and threw it over their face so they could drift in and out of sleep for the next hour until giving in to the daybreak, and headed into the bathroom.

New start means not looking homeless, The Outsider thought, while staring, unimpressed, at a face in the mirror: an unkempt beard and long dark brown hair, no longer the style he suited. He got in the shower and planned his list.

Buy an electric razor. Let's start from skin-head? Or will people look at me like I'm an ex-con? he contemplated.

Okay, maybe that isn't the best plan. But still I have to do something about this beard at least.

He turned the shower off and dripped for a few seconds.

A towel, shampoo, toothpaste. Toiletries in general, you're not living out the backseat of the car anymore, be civilized. He tied up his hair with the elastic band around his wrist.

His first stop was the supermarket: fruit, veg, carbs, pasta, snacks, toiletries. Then the home-ware store: electric razor, pots, pans, cutlery, plates, microwave, toaster, some blankets, blow-up mattress, and pillows. The Girl at the counter scanned the first item then began her small talk.

"Moving in?" she asked.

"Yep."

"Thought you looked unfamiliar. I get used to seeing the same faces around here." She scanned the razor and looked up at him, her curious eyes focused on his beard. "New faces are definitely welcome, at least in my opinion," she said with her signature smile, warm and welcoming, yet devious and suggestive.

She had shoulder-length, dark hair with a block fringe. Hazel eyes, a small nose with freckles scattered across it, and a drawn-on beauty mark on the top left corner of her lip allured yet concerned The Outsider.

He pulled his wallet out to start counting the cash while she scanned the last few items.

"Do you know anyone around here then?" Her customer service smile could have been mistaken for flirtatious.

"I briefly met the owner of The Cafe at the end of town. I've moved into the apartment above."

"Mick, such a sweet man, and the cutest little girl." She pointed to her badge as she printed the receipt and said, "Well, I'm Brooke. I usually work the midday shifts, so am free most afternoons and evenings." That smile of hers formed. "If you need someone to show you around all the secret little spots in this town, feel free to message me."

She wrote her number on the back of his receipt and put it into one of the bags.

"Have a good day, sir."

As he pushed the cart away, he turned back to see her look over while serving the next customer and give him one more of her smiles.

Next stop, clothes: underwear, socks, and a towel, of course. New shoes, white jeans, blue jeans, another hoodie, and a button-up shirt.

With 10:00 fast approaching and his stomach starting to

cramp, it was time for breakfast at The Cafe. He parked and took everything upstairs to the apartment, debating if he should unpack the bags, but his stomach got the better of him.

The Cafe windows were decorated with hanging plants. A mother and her daughter sat at a table outside enjoying the sunny spring day. Inside, half the tables were seated; one was being cleared by The Waitress. Our Outsider chose a table by the window. He smiled at Mick who was serving at the counter.

"Good morning, Mick," said The Outsider as he sat down.

"Good morning ... I'm so sorry I've forgotten your name."

"It's fine, we didn't actually exchange names. I bought some stuff from the home-ware store this morning and the girl on the counter told me yours."

"Dark hair and freckles?"

"Brooke, yes."

Michael curled up his mouth. "Very friendly girl. Always the talk of the town."

There was an awkward pause before The Outsider held out his hand.

"Blaine. Sorry I'm a little late."

"No worries at all. You've got to get settled and from what you said yesterday sounds like you probably had a lot of stuff to get this morning."

"Yes, I did. I've bought a razor to tidy up the mess that is my face," Blaine said.

"Have a look through the menu and I'll send Vanessa over in a second."

"Thank you again for this." Blaine picked up the menu.

"We are neighbours now, want you to feel welcome." Michael walked over to the counter.

Blaine flicked through the menu, starved but not wanting

to overstep the invite. He gazed out the window and watched the mother and daughter draw and giggle.

"So I hear you're the guy who's moved in upstairs?" a confident voice said from nearby the table.

"I'm famous. Seems everyone knows me," Blaine replied.

"The famous outsider, all know his title, none know his story."

Vanessa was cute. Dimples in her smile, big emerald eyes, and blonde hair tied up in a bun with two strands flowing down and framing her face.

"I'm sure rumours of my story will spread just as quickly as news of my arrival did."

"This is a small town and a mysterious man arrives from nowhere with nothing. Can you blame people for being excited and curious about why?"

"I guess not. I am kind of a big deal," he replied and she rolled her eyes back at him as they laughed.

"So what can I get for you? Mick says it's on the house."

"Full English and a glass of orange juice, please."

"All good, I'll put that through for you." She turned with a hop.

This really is a small town if my arrival has stirred up this much fuss already. He continued to watch the woman and her daughter as Vanessa brought over the juice.

"That's Jenny, Mick's wife, and their daughter Sam," Vanessa said.

"Everyone seems so happy here."

"You're new. From the outside this is a lovely town, but if you stay long enough you'll start to see its flaws."

"Controversial."

She chuckled, then whispered, "Shh. Don't tell anyone. They all want you to think it is perfect here."

Blaine smiled, "Nothing is perfect. That's what makes it real."

Vanessa was softly fixated on him. "Wise words from the mystery man."

They locked eyes as he spoke. "Not wise, just observant."

"How old are you?" The words left her mouth without her permission.

"Much younger than I look."

Vanessa's posture shrunk. "Sorry, that was a bit personal."

"We're neighbours now; we probably should get to know each other. I'm twenty-four."

"That is younger than I thought. I figured you were about twenty-seven." A surprised look on her face but also a sense of relief, her body still tense.

"Yeah, I know, I'm not aging well," Blaine said.

"No, that's not what I meant, I ..."

He chuckled and relaxed into his seat with a forgiving smile. "It's fine. I get it all the time, it's just the beard and hair. I've bought a razor. First order of business is sorting that out."

"Yeah, the ponytail is an interesting choice." Vanessa's confidence returned.

Blaine tipped his head to the side and nodded in acceptance, laughing out of his nose.

After the breakfast Mick took Blaine outside to introduce him to Sam and Jenny. There was lots of small talk and niceties, but all Blaine could think of was, *They want you to think it's perfect here.*

"Thank you again for the breakfast." He shook Mick's hand.

"My pleasure, you seem like a very charming guy and you're attracting a lot of attention already."

"Especially from the ladies, it seems," Jenny added.

"Well, what can I say, I have that effect," Blaine joked.

"I can imagine, especially once you sort that hair out," Mick said.

"Next on the list. Believe me!"

The ponytail was the first part to go, then it was grade six all over. It didn't look bad; it didn't look good. Next to go was the beard. He left the moustache and laughed at himself in the mirror for a few minutes before then shaving that too. He went from twenty-seven, down to looking nineteen.

Wait for the stubble to grow back a bit then it'll look perfect.

He sorted through everything he had bought before heading back out for some more kitchen supplies and things that sprung to mind as essentials.

As the evening rolled on, he completely forgot about the sunset at the courts, so promised himself to do that tomorrow. He cooked pasta, served it up with a jar of tomato sauce, and sat on the counter to eat while looking at the bare apartment.

After washing up, Blaine blew up the air mattress.

Tomorrow is the beginning of a new chapter. Hopefully it will be a good one. Guess the best place to start would be looking for a job.

He unpacked the blankets, changed into a pair of new underwear, and slowly drifted off to sleep.

~~~

Welcome.

To a story that will show you a truth, hidden in your own mind. Welcome to a story of change, of finding purpose, soul, and life. It's a story that shows the lost, the wandering, or the idle that if you approach life true to yourself, you will find direction. To those who are weighted by titles that no longer fit their names, it gives the opportunity to grow and discover who they could become.

It is written with the intention that you look deeper, not just within the story, but within yourself. This story is full of wisdoms and secrets that, if approached with a curious mind, will reveal beauty in the smallest of details.

The Town

Day broke through the window and woke him early once more. He dragged the blanket over his face and just like yesterday continued to dream, before making his way into the bathroom. Blaine's reflection was new, young, and refreshing. He cracked a smile at the bad haircut, brushed his teeth, and had a good shower. He put on the white jeans, the new hoodie, and made breakfast.

"A job ... you need a job," he said as he served up his omelette. "Retail, labor work, hospitality, storeroom, anything. You need to start making some money before you run out again."

Blaine wandered around the town centre, popping in and out of stores, introducing himself to more people. He asked if any were hiring, but wasn't having the best luck. Some offered part-time hours, which he considered, but was looking for something full-time.

While job hunting, he bought a few things to make the apartment homely: knick-knacks for the kitchen, a cactus to put in the window, and a mug. Around 3:00 he decided to call it a day and try again tomorrow at the restaurants instead, so he walked home.

As he approached, he acknowledged the sign that was being pushed by the breeze. "The Cafe." He stifled a laugh. *Guess there isn't much competition.*

Blaine walked through the door and was greeted by Vanessa. "You look good!"

"Thanks." Blaine smiled.

"You have such a great face. Seriously. The beard hides it so much. But the hair!"

"I did my best, but yes, I know. Luckily no one has said anything."

Vanessa didn't try to hide her laughter. "Because they are being nice. Grab a seat, I'll get you a jug of water." They chatted about the town and the people he'd had to introduce himself to.

Blaine asked Vanessa about herself and found out she modelled for extra cash.

"No surprise you model, easy money for you," he said.

"I should get back to it."

She took his order and left him to watch the world go by, while she went back to her work. Mick and Vanessa talked about Blaine in the kitchen with the chef, Dean.

"He is so charming!" Vanessa spied through the kitchen door window.

"Has someone got a crush?" Mick nudged her, handing her a towel to dry some plates and cutlery.

"Maybe a little, but can you blame me?"

"He's just new and interesting. Give it a few days of him coming in here and you'll get bored," Dean pitched in, trying to peer past Vanessa's head. "He's not even that attractive, it's just the fact he is different. I mean, what's with that haircut?"

Vanessa giggled to herself and continued polishing cutlery before she went back out to serve Blaine and clear tables. As she cleared, she kept looking over to Blaine. He caught her eye and gave a gesture for the bill. She nodded and went behind the counter to print it.

She handed it to him and playfully added, "Actually going to pay today, huh?"

He scoffed at the comment. "Yeah, and even tip you for the conversation."

"That costs nothing." Her dimples showed.

"Well, in that case, give it to the chef. Chefs rarely get the appreciation they deserve."

"What's your plan for the rest of the afternoon then?"

"I made myself a promise to watch the sunset from The Basketball Court up the road. I'll run upstairs and grab my MP3 player and headphones, then chill there for a bit."

Vanessa's dimples formed. "MP3 player ... woah."

"I know. I told you I'm not aging well. I just don't have a phone at the moment."

"I didn't realise people still used them, but that sounds wonderful. Well, enjoy your evening and hopefully see you tomorrow?"

"No doubt you will."

Blaine waved to Mick, catching Dean's eye. He winked and then left. Vanessa cashed off his bill and walked into the kitchen with the change.

"Why'd he wink at me?" Dean gruffed.

She chuckled and took her hand out of her pocket, showing him the change. "He tipped you."

"He can't charm me that easily."

Mick patted Dean on the back. "Lighten up, he seems like a decent guy."

~~~

A beautiful spring evening, the third now after a long, wet winter. Our Outsider, Blaine, sat alone under the hoop of The Basketball Court — Blink-182 playing through headphones, a cool spring breeze warmed by the sunset.

He sat reflecting. It had been a long time since he had been welcomed anywhere, let alone welcomed warmly.

Blaine twiddled The Feather Necklace that he kept tucked under his shirt. It was a copper pendant, turning green from age, on a thin silver chain. Watching the sky, his thoughts wandered. It was only the end of day two and he knew what he was like, always finding ways to screw things up. As the sun teetered above the horizon, he felt someone approach him from the other side of the court. He moved a headphone to the side and looked over.

"You're still here? I thought you'd have gone by now." Vanessa spoke from the half-court line.

"The sun's not finished setting yet."

"What have you been doing?"

"Just thinking."

"About?" she asked again.

"Life." He smiled at the sunset.

"Deep." Vanessa tucked her skirt under herself as she sat beside him. "Do you mind if I join?" He shuffled over.

Vanessa's gaze stayed fixed on the sunset. "You know I can sort your hair out for you if you like?"

"Is it that bad?"

"Well no ... It's okay. But I can make you look much better than okay."

He turned to her and said, "Can I trust you?"

"More than you should have trusted yourself," she smirked.

"Sure."

"Now?"

"After the sunset."

They both sat quiet, leaning on their arms, close enough their hands could almost touch. As the sun fell below the trees, Blaine rose to his feet and held out his hand to help Vanessa to hers. Her hair touched her dimples and she brushed the gravel from her skirt.

He unlocked the apartment door, apologising for the lack of everything, and explained how he wasn't expecting to have any guests for a while, if ever.

Blaine offered her water, pouring it into The Mug. "It's the only one I have. I got it today," he explained.

"Mick was right. You really don't have anything, do you?"

"Fresh start," Blaine said quietly, tired of hearing himself say it.

"And you really don't say much when you're alone, do you? Is the Mr Charming I've met downstairs all just an act then?"

"Maybe I'm nervous now that it's just us."

She blushed, turning away to smile, and put The Mug down on the kitchen counter.

"Right, so how are we going to do this?" Vanessa stood next to him, her head barely coming up to his chin.

"I can kneel?"

"A bit too soon for that," she sniggered. It caught Blaine off guard. "It might work? Just would be a bit uncomfortable for you."

He dropped down on one knee in front of her. Vanessa laughed and shook her head, then, plugging in the razor, began. They both laughed each time Blaine adjusted his legs to work through the discomfort.

Blaine couldn't remember the last time he had felt relaxed with someone like this. Well, he could, but tried not to.

"Ahh, my masterpiece! It is finished!" Vanessa switched the razor off, dragged him to his feet, and led him to the bathroom.

A handsome, tidy, face greeted him in the mirror, hair short on back and sides. It shocked him.

"Woah! It's ... how did ... How?" He couldn't stop smiling at his reflection. "I look good."

Yes, you do, Vanessa thought.

"Thank you!" he said, stroking the back of his head. "You seem surprised. I told you I'm good."

"Not just for the haircut. Thank you for making me feel welcome and for spending your evening here. You could have been somewhere else."

"Honestly," she said, following him out of the bathroom, "I should be thanking you for giving me a reason not to go home. My parents drive me mad."

"You live with your parents?"

"Yeah. I've been saving up and trying to figure out what to do with my life. Twenty, nearly twenty-one, and still living at home, working the same job I've been at since sixteen."

"There's nothing wrong with that at all. Life isn't a race. There's no rush."

"Easy for you, Mr I've-travelled-and-done-so-much."

"Yeah, and look what I have to show for it." He gestured around the room. "But I guess life comes and it goes. As long as you're walking, nothing is stopping you from changing direction and wandering to a new place."

"Is that what you'll do if you don't like it here?"

"It's what I've done in the past. But, it's different here." He continued. "There is something about it that makes me want to stick around. I trust my instincts." He cracked a smile as he saw Vanessa pick up The Mug and take a drink. "That's why I bought a mug."

Vanessa, mid-sip, snorted the water. They both burst into laughter, then she composed herself. "So The Mug is a symbol of home?"

"Yeah. A mug is a symbol of a place you belong. Everyone has that special mug and that special place it sits."

Vanessa's phone rang. Her parents. It was nearly 10:00. On that note she left.

That night Blaine spent a few minutes longer looking in the mirror, smiling at the haircut, before blowing some more air into the mattress and falling asleep.

~~~

Now I'm going to skip past all this next part, dear reader. He bought a phone, found a job, filled out all the boring paperwork and admin stuff, and started two days later. So we've jumped past the formal interview stuff, his repetitive introductions to the people in town and people at work, and instead we go straight to the place Our Outsider starts to change his title and become The Insider.

But will changing this title change his skin and his role? Does that change his effect on the story? Does it remove the effect of his past? Change the person he was? Or does this fresh start end up the same as all the others - a packed bag, leaving in the middle of the night with no explanation, just an apology on a note?

The Insider

The next few weeks were repetitive and routine for Blaine. Bites to eat at The Cafe before just before noon, work in the evenings. Days off were spent shopping for decorations to make the apartment more comfortable. Some spent with Vanessa.

Blaine found out she was a nerd in high school: got good grades; loved sci-fi stuff, comic books, and music. She played trumpet in a band before she realised it was uncool; her being pretty meant she should become a cheerleader instead.

Rather than spending money going to University to study something she didn't enjoy, Vanessa decided to stay at home with her parents. He admitted to dropping out for the same reason.

She'd ask him on occasion about the past, but he'd danced around the questions.

"But surely that breeds rumours?"

"But rumours are rumours," Blaine said as they walked through town. "People can play with the idea of them all they like, they know it's not the truth. Plus the rumours people come up with entertain me."

Blaine became a familiar face in The Town, the curious looks fading. Working at the bar, Kestrel, helped. He was always chatty when making drinks and serving.

It was the fourth Monday since he moved in. For the first time, the sun did not wake him. On his own, he opened his eyes, rolled off the blow-up bed, drew the new curtains, and walked over to the wardrobe. It was a warm day so he grabbed a pair of shorts and a baggy tank top and went into the bathroom, now decorated with rocks, a tub of coco butter, moisturizers, soaps, and shower gels. Brushing his teeth using charcoal toothpaste, he studied his beard, ready to be taken back to stubble.

He had to be at work for 12:00 to stock check and receive deliveries. He made himself a bowl of cereal and sat by the window.

He left the apartment, said a quick hello to Vanessa who was outside serving, and put his headphones on, listening to Jack's Mannequin.

~~~

Kestrel was a big bar, one of the main spots, with a bigger dancefloor than The Rabbit Hole and Thieves Den. Also it had an upstairs balcony area, unlike Mark and Charlie.

The top bar had become Blaine's position on weekends. His new face and charming personality, Tim had noticed, made people keen to chat. He was settling into the role of bartender-therapist, bringing people back for more drinks.

Tim was a good businessman. Now in his early forties, he had experience running and managing clubs in big cities.

When his father died six years ago, Tim had come home for the funeral to discover his father had left him his old gym building. So he opened Kestrel, named after the bird that hovers before it strikes.

"We needed a pretty male face on the bar," he said to Blaine. "Well, a young pretty male face." Tim checked his reflection in a glass. "See, that's the sad thing with this business. It's shallow. People want to be served their drinks by a face that's worth coming back to." He hinted over to Amanda. She was tall and athletic, with a pretty face and big assets. "Boobs sell beer. And it's sad that I have to exploit it. But, at the end of the day, it works."

Amanda chimed in, "The attention is kind of nice anyway, right? I just play the character they think I am, wait until they believe they are getting somewhere, and then have the pleasure of deflating their ego. Rinse and repeat every weekend. It's the small pleasures in life."

"You're a perfect addition, mate." Tim continued, "There are fuck loads of newly divorced ladies looking to relive their youth. I can flirt with them all I like, but they want someone the age that they are trying to be. And let's face it, that ain't me no more. But just as the older women like the younger guys, the younger girls want an older man, and that's my clientele."

You knew Tim had hair on his chest in all the right places, and smooth skin and muscle tone in the rest. Clean shaven, occasionally bristly, and dark brown eyes. Tall, fit, and for any girl with the slightest of daddy issues, a definite treat.

~~~

Blaine walked through the double doors and took his head phones off.

"Yo, B. Give us a hand bringing some kegs through, would ya," Tim called out.

By 5:00 Amanda showed up to swap over.

"What are your plans for this evening?" Amanda asked as Blaine got his coat.

"Might eat out. I haven't been shopping so figured I'd try that Italian near the high school."

"Alone?"

"Yeah?"

"I could never eat out alone," she confessed, then raised an eyebrow. "So you've not met anyone yet? None of the girls you flirt with given you their numbers?"

He remembered the girl he met on the first day in the homeware but must have thrown the receipt away before he got his phone.

"There's a girl who works below me ..." He broke off, hearing the words come out of his mouth.

"I bet she does," Amanda laughed.

"Ha ha. No, in The Cafe. But you know. Don't shit where you eat, quite literally."

"Vanessa Gretchen? She is a stunner. Quiet little thing, though."

"Seriously, how does everyone know everyone?"

"You're quite known as well, my friend," she teased. "I babysat her when I was sixteen, this adorable little nine year old nerdy girl. Puberty hits, so do boys and parties. After that, rumours spread about her, I think, and she turned back into that quiet girl I used to babysit. Shame really."

The walk home was windy. As he got close to The Cafe, he saw Vanessa locking up. She hadn't noticed him and started to walk away, so he called out to her. She didn't hear him the first time but did the second.

"Are you all good, Blaine?"

"Yeah, just wanted to catch you before you left."

"Oh, that's sweet." She avoided eye contact.

"I was thinking of eating out tonight. I'd usually just go alone but I saw you closing and thought it might be nice to have some company."

"I'd really like that. But I want to go home and shower first. What time would you want to go?"

"Around 8:00?"

"Yeah, okay. But if you want to be a bit fashionably late, I'd appreciate that."

"I could take you home now if you want."

He dropped her at the end of her road then drove back to the apartment to shower and get dressed, putting on the blue jeans and the nice shirt, leaving the top button open, The Feather Necklace just visible.

Fashionably late. I'll leave just after 8:00.

His phone pinged at 7:45 - Vanessa: I'll be ready in 5 if u wanna leave now?

As Blaine pulled up outside, before he could even turn the engine off, she came out the door. Her mother peeked through the blind.

Vanessa was wearing a short denim skirt, with black tights, knee-high boots and a Jack's Mannequin T-shirt under an embroidered denim jacket.

Beaming her dimpled smile, she opened the car door. "Hey! Thanks for the invite and for getting me out of the house."

"Looks like she wants to join you?" Blaine nodded towards the window and waved.

"She's the worst. She was like to Gareth, 'The new man is taking your daughter on a date,' and he just grumbled, 'He better be paying.' … I really don't get out much." She gritted her teeth.

Blaine set off.

"So your partying days are behind you, I hear." Vanessa went stiff. "I got the gossip off Amanda that you used to be a, and I quote, 'party animal' back in high school."

"Oh god, Amanda. I forgot you worked with her! What did she tell you?"

"Just that you liked to party. Past tense."

"So, she didn't give you any details?"

"Nope. It was a brief conversation." He peered over at her, anxious in the seat beside him.

"Sorry, I was just playing. I mean, you know how I look at the past. It's been and gone, none of my business. Also backtrack, so your parents think this is a date?"

"Boy and a girl going out to dinner? Of course she does."

"Does this mean I get to kiss you when I drop you home?"

She laughed, and slapped his arm. "Depends on how much of a gentleman you are tonight."

"Great start then?" he said, sucking his teeth.

"Yeah, really great start."

They arrived at the Italian, ordering drinks straight away. He peered at her shirt and said, "This night's a perfect shade of dark blue."

Vanessa looked out the window. "It is, isn't it."

"Have you ever been alone in a crowded room?"

"Ohhh," she sighed. "My T-shirt!"

"Good. You're not just one of those girls that wears random band T's she doesn't know."

"Of course not! I'm offended you'd think that. But I'll forgive you because I'm impressed."

"I was listening to that album today, funnily enough."

"No way! How weird. Okay, favourite songs off the album?"

"Dark Blue, hence the first lyric in my head. You?"

"Miss Delaney! They have so many good songs! That's crazy, I love Jack's Mannequin!"

"Then you've got good taste in music. Give me pop punk and all that angst-y teen stuff from the early 00s."

Vanessa's eyes lit up. "Literally!"

They both ordered pasta dishes, making the common lady and the tramp joke, and continued talking about music from their teen years.

Blaine paid for the bill and they left, walking so close their arms kept brushing. Vanessa watched her feet. "I'm really glad you moved here. Honestly. You've brought some eventfulness back into my life."

"Good, I'm glad. I'm glad I met someone like you straight away. I wouldn't usually decorate an apartment this early."

"Or buy a mug?"

"Or buy a mug." He took a deep breath. "I could settle here."

"Well, personally, I really hope you do."

They drove home, both quietly singing along to Blaine's CD player hooked up in the car – You Me At Six, Take off Your Colours. As he pulled up outside Vanessa's house, she thanked him again for the invitation and she got out, hesitating to shut the door. He leaned across the gear-stick. Vanessa ducked her head back in to kiss him on the cheek.

"It was a really great date," she whispered.

He smiled and whispered back, "She's at the blinds again."

"Good. Let her gossip." Taking her hand from his shoulder, she shut the door and walked towards the house.

"Bye!" Blaine shouted as she stepped inside.

Blaine showed up for his shift, greeted by, "So, you and pretty li'l Miss Gretchen?" Tim raised an eyebrow, his tongue protruding through his grin.

"Whoa! Rumours do spread like wildfire in this town, don't they!"

"Amanda told me you went out to dinner on Monday."

"And how does Amanda know this?" Blaine said as Amanda joined them behind the bar.

"Her mother called me asking for a reference. Vanessa told her you worked here."

Tim took a tray of clean glasses from the washer and began to polish. "So you told her he's an ex-convict, yeah?"

"This town needs to find something to talk about other

than me." Blaine paused. "Do people think I'm an ex-convict?" Tim shook his head and mimed, *I'm playing.*

"I told her he is one of the nice guys. Hard working and genuine ... with a mysterious past." Blaine nodded in agreement.

~~~

He woke up the next morning around ten, rolled off the blow-up mattress, and threw a hoodie on to go down for breakfast. After he sat down at his usual table, Jenny walked over with a notepad and pen, and wearing an apron.

"They've got you working today, then?" he asked.

"Yeah, Mick's parents are in town so he is spending the day with them and Sam, and Vanessa is out of town for a modelling job. So that leaves me. Sorry."

"No, it's a pleasant change. Gives me a chance to chat with you and find out who Jenny is."

"No wonder Vanessa is smitten with you when you sweet talk like that."

"Is she now?"

He finished breakfast and went back up to continue reading his book about a world where drugs link dreams.

When he arrived for his shift just before 5:30, Mel, queen of cocktails, already had a group of girls lining up shots at the downstairs bar. He headed upstairs to his and Amanda's bar for the night.

"It's 5:30, right?" he asked as he hung his coat around the back.

Amanda laughed, "Yup!"

"Jeez! There is a group of girls already on tequila shots downstairs."

"You're surprised? If you were a student and went back to your town, what would you do?"

"Drin-," he stopped himself. "I see your point."

"Plus, they are all trying to prove how much they can drink now. So strap in, Boyo. It's gonna get messy."

"Great! Looking forward to it. Tips should be good, though."

"Students don't tip."

"Not you, maybe …"

"Oh! Oh, okay, it's on!" A guy walked up to the bar. "We'll compare at the end of the shift."

The guy caught the end of the comment. "What are you comparing?"

"Dick sizes. I said I reckon yours is bigger." Amanda said.

Blaine scoffed and walked to the other end of the bar. And so the competition began. It helped to pass the time. Before they knew it, 8:00 rolled by and Kestrel was full. Shot after shot, beer after beer, girl after girl asking Blaine when he moved to town.

"Right, that's not fair, you have an advantage," Amanda quibbled after the tenth girl had tipped him.

Blaine coughed "Boobs!" as his retort. Amanda shook the cocktail she was preparing.

She looked down and smiled. "Point taken."

By 10:00 most people were downstairs dancing. Only a few came up to get drinks instead of waiting in the queue by the dancefloor bar. There was a quiet moment so they had a rough count in their pockets

"Twenty-five?" Blaine said.

"Really? Damn, yeah, I'm about the same."

A girl came running over to the bar and called out, "New guy! You never gave me your name!"

He noticed the freckles across her nose and then the penciled beauty mark.

"Brooke, right?"

"Yeah! You never called." She pushed her bottom lip out into a false frown.

"Yeah, sorry, I didn't have a phone then."

"What kind of excuse is that?" As she spoke, a guy came over to her and put his arm around her waist. "Danny, this is the famous new guy!"

"Famous?" Danny screwed up his face.

"Blaine." He held out his hand. Danny shook with a masculine grip, so Blaine gripped tighter.

Danny turned to Brooke. "Babe, me and the boys are going back over to Mark and Charlie. It's dead in here."

Brooke clenched her teeth, then smiled. "Have fun! The girls and I are staying here so we can dance."

"Cool, ring me later, yeah? Whenever you're ready to go back to mine." Danny left before waiting for an answer.

She sighed. "My Knight. How lucky am I." Wincing, she gulped down the last of her drink. "Double vanilla vodka on ice? Pleasssee." She screwed up her eyes and gave him a toothy smile.

He poured her drink. "Boys, huh."

"Ugh. Tell me about it … So what are you, a man? Because I could do with one of those." She touched his hand as she took the drink from him.

"Nope, also a boy. That's how I know."

Brooke giggled at Blaine's dismissal. He poked a straw into the glass and she pinched it, bringing it to her lips.

"He comes back for a few days. I haven't seen him in months, and he goes off with 'the boys,' then just expects me to go sleep at his later. We aren't even really together anymore … I don't even know why I bother."

"You're young, too young to put up needlessly with stuff like that."

"Yeah. I know … Sorry. I don't know why I …"

"It's fine. Bartenders make for cheap therapy. Everyone knows that."

She perked up, grabbing a tip and something else from her purse. "Cheap, yes. But it shouldn't be free." She held out her hand so he held his out, too. She put the tip in his hand, holding it so she could write on his wrist with a pen. They locked eyes and Brooke said, "Call me this time, okay?"

She let go, winked, and walked away towards the stairs, turning back to call over, "I like the haircut."

1:30 rolled around and the upstairs bar closed. Whoever was left now was downstairs dancing until close. While clearing, Amanda and Blaine compared their final tip count.

"Fifty!" Blaine said.

"Fifty? I only got forty … Fair play, mate. I'll give you that one. This was fun! Next big event we should play this little game again, yeah?"

They shook hands. "If I can get fifty in one night, then definitely!"

The night ended, leaving Blaine to sort out the bar, while Amanda cleaned the tables. She brought over a tray of glasses and he loaded them into the washer.

"The girl who wrote that number on your arm, Brooke Bennett, be careful with her, okay? Don't get stuck in the middle of anything."

The Princess

The next morning, day broke through the window. Out of bed she rolled and stumbled to the bathroom. The face in the mirror was heavy, the night before had been long and stressful. *Same again tonight ... same old shit.*

She stumbled back to the room, picking up clothes scattered over the floor, peering, ashamed, at the body asleep in the bed as she dressed and left out the back door of the bedroom.

Our Princess walked down the street, back to her own home.

Fuck sake why did you do this.

She walked up in the driveway and crept into the house. The sun rested on the horizon. She went up to her room and crashed on the bed, wrapped herself in the duvet, and fell back to sleep.

The sun now at its peak, her head still lay buried beneath the covers.

"I know your friends are all back but you're not spending the whole weekend like this," her mother called through the door. "Get up, sort yourself out, and get to work before you're late. Those friends of yours are bad influences. You are finally getting yourself together. Don't let them bring you back down."

Our Princess groaned, rolled back out of bed, and headed into the bathroom. Messy bed head still not any better, but at least her hazel eyes were now able to open wider. She showered, drew on her beauty mark, and put on her home-ware store uniform. Checking her phone, she realized she had only ten minutes until she had to be at work. And she had unread texts.

> 9:10 - Danny: why did u leave without wakin me
>
> 10:23 - Danny: we good?
>
> 10:27 - Work: Any chance you can start at 12 today?
>
> 10:37 - Danny: Was gdbein with u again last night missed this missed u missed us
>
> 11:53 - Katie: I'm hanging out my ass
>
> 11:53 - Katie: gurlll you can still drink!! what time you finish work? I'll pick you up and we can get ready at mine
>
> 11:54 - Katie: I wanna look hot af I AM going home with that new bartender at Kestrel tonight

Fuck sake ... FUCK SAKE! Why can't you just sort your shit out and keep it that way ... Why are you so self-destructive? she thought as she rubbed her face.

"Because it's fun," she whispered to herself, smiling back at the mirror before running downstairs.

"Hi! Bye!"

"Brooke! You're going to be late."

"I start at 1:00. It's fine."

"That's in five minutes. You can't walk there in five minutes."

Our Princess didn't reply.

Her mother groaned. "Take the car. I'll walk into town and pick it up later." Brooke gave her a kiss on the cheek as she got to her feet. "Where were you 'til eight this morning, anyway? Did you not stay the whole night with Katie?"

"Actually I slept at Danny's," she mumbled.

"You slept where!" Her father had overheard from around the corner.

"BYE! Love you!" She grabbed the keys and ran out the door.

Brooke clocked in at 1:02.

"Good night, then?" said her manager as she walked past, still wearing her sunglasses.

"Yup. Same again tonight, so no text tomorrow asking me to come in, 'kay?" She pulled the sunglasses down to wink at him.

"How's Katharine?"

"Still out of your league!" she shouted back without stopping to turn.

The Princess put her bag and the sunglasses in her locker, tied on her apron, and sat behind the cash register. Four hours of meaningless scanning and small talk. The boredom hurt so much she forgot all about the hangover.

She texted Katie: pick me up @6:30. bring vanilla vodka

The rest of the shift rolled by, and she clocked out at 6:29, leaving the staff room just as Katie walked in. The Manager walked over to her with open arms. "Welcome home, Katharine. We've missed having you here."

"I bet you have, Eddy. Place must be boring without me around. Come for a drink at Kestrel tonight, yeah?"

"I finish at … "

"Yeah okay, Boo. Hey Brookie, vodka is in the car. Let's go, girl!"

Brooke walked past the manager. "Bye Eddy. See you Monday."

"Are you sure you … " Eddy started, but both walked out without turning back and shouted out, "Nope!" with a pop.

They jumped in Katie's father's jet black Triumph TR6 convertible and Brooke grabbed the bottle of vodka out of the footwell. When her father wasn't home, what he didn't know couldn't hurt him. They decided first to head to the hill that overlooked the neighbouring town.

As they pulled up, the sun floated low in the sky. Brooke took another sip of the vodka.

"So how is it I'm the one who parties, yet you're the one who can still outdrink me?"

Brooke guzzled the vodka, most of her face hidden under her sunglasses. "It's just practice, Boo."

"So you and Danny back together? Or just fuckin'?"

Brooke stopped drinking abruptly and screwed the top back on. "Neither … Dude was too drunk and just passed out when we got in. I thought he'd grow up a bit but, no, he gains more jerk points … I'm not wasting my time with him tonight."

"Sexy bartender?"

"Tempting, but rumour in town is him and Gretchen have a little thing."

Katie cackled. "Jeez, you and that girl's lives are intertwined, I swear."

Brooke unscrewed the cap. "Yeah, so let's not relive the past, shall we." She took another sip.

~~~

After 9:30, they entered Mark and Charlie, their friends already crowding the bar. Danny sidled up, put his hands around her waist, and kissed her on the neck. "Hey, babe."

"Hi Dan."

"You never text me back. Why'd you leave this morning?"

She pushed his hands away and turned around to lean on the bar. "Dan … I'm not doing this."

"Doing what?" he flirted.

Her smile dropped away. "Us. Dan, I'm not doing us. These games aren't fun for me anymore, they just waste energy. I could have gone straight home to my own bed." She dropped to a whisper. "Admittedly I was drunk and a little horny. But when I woke up, the excitement I used to get was gone." She ordered her drinks and paid.

"So … what does this mean?" He took a step back.

"It means, my lovely Danny, I'm sleeping in my own bed. You're free to do as you want tonight, and every other night you're home. I'm done playing this game with you. We are over." She picked the drinks up and stood on her tiptoes to kiss him on the cheek. "Enjoy your future, Boo. It's been fun." Brooke walked over to the group.

Part of the group, including Danny, stayed in Mark and Charlie, while Brooke and Katie and the rest had a round of shots and went to Kestrel. As they walked in, Katie nudged Brooke, noticing that Our Insider was working on the downstairs bar across from the dance floor. Katie walked towards the edge of the floor and danced, emphasising every part she knew to be her best feature.

Brooke laughed deeply, a genuine belly laugh, at her friend whose outfit made the boys forgive that fact that she clearly could not dance. She skipped over to join Katie.

Blaine noticed the two of them dancing, let's just say to their own beat. He caught Katie's eye. She approached the bar to order a cider and a double vodka neat.

"So you're the new cute bartender I keep hearing about?"

"Seriously, this town needs to find something new to talk about. I've been here a month now. You're Brooke's friend?" He handed her the bottles.

She took a sip. "Yeah! So you've met?"

He showed her the faded number on his wrist. "She's given me her number twice."

"Well, maybe you should call it then."

~~~

Light crept in gently through The Princess's blinds as noon made itself known. A knock at the door followed by, "Brooke

Bethany Bennett, if you want breakfast before it becomes lunch you better make your way downstairs soon!" The smell of bacon flowed under the door. She rolled over and reached for her bottle of water, took a sip, put it back on her bedside table, and replaced it with her phone.

> 4:43 - Danny: bed is cold without u;)
> 10:26 - Unknown: Thought it was about time I messaged you. If you're not too hung-over maybe you could show me one of those secret spots you spoke about before?
> 11:01 - Katie: how the fuck did I get home last night? whats this dudes name?

Thought it was about time I messaged you? Who is ... NO!!
She sat up straight. *Fuck off!* She unlocked her phone and replied to Katie.

> Message sent: Blonde guy or really short guy? Also guess who text me!?!?!

She sat on the edge of her bed, looking at her outfit from the night before, abandoned in a trail from the door, then pushed herself to her feet, and walked into the bathroom. Face of smudged eyeliner, messy black hair, a bra clinging on by one hook, strap fallen down over her shoulder, underwear bunched up. She made herself presentable and put on an oversized pink fluffy hoodie. Her phone buzzed.

> 11:09 - Katie: Not blonde so short? And Danny?
> She typed back: dunno then we just called him Shawty.
> And yeah but no I'm done with those games. Bartender guy!! Sent@11:10

She stumbled downstairs and sat up on the kitchen counter, grabbing an apple from the fruit bowl.

"Good night?" asked her father, turning the bacon.

She breathed in. "Yeah. Smells good!"

He raised a brow. "Danny?"

"I'm done playing those games. I'm a big girl now, Dad!" she said, biting into the apple.

"Barely," he scoffed. "Pay me some rent and I'll consider giving you that title. Not hungover, then?"

She gasped at the comment, smiled, took the bacon out of the pan, and put it on the slice of buttered bread. Her father chuckled.

"That's my girl."

Her phone buzzed - Katie: ffs fuck it Imma just roll him out the bed

It buzzed again: No. FCUKING. WAYYY! What did he say?!

"Katie trying to figure out how to get a boy out of her bed again?" asked her father, watching her giggle at her phone as she took a bite of the sandwich.

She let out a deep belly laugh, sending Katie:

He wants to meet me today!!

"Yeah, her Shawty," she said, mimicking a very bad 90s rap voice and wrist flick.

Handing her another sandwich, he sighed, "Call her and pass me the phone."

She quickly typed: hero dad, loud speaker

And swapped him the phone for the plate.

It rang for a few seconds and then, "JENIFER! I AM ON MY WAY HOME. I SWEAR TO GOD IF THERE IS A BOY IN THAT BED THEN ALL THREE OF US ARE GOING TO HAVE A VERY LONG TALK!" And her father hung up. Brooke sniggered while eating the sandwich. "That used to make Danny run a mile."

"Ohhh, the mysterious Jenifer. It works every time."

A group of the girls used to go by "Jenifer" when they went to parties to confuse the boys. The mysterious Jenifer gained quite the reputation before the secret got out. But "Jenifering" still worked.

After breakfast, she showered, tried on a few different outfits, did her make-up, added the beauty mark, and settled on a pair of black boots, leggings, knee-length black skirt and a thin yellow long-sleeved turtleneck. Ready for Blaine at 4:00.

"You look nice," her mother said, passing her in the corridor. "Isn't that what you wore to the festival after-party last year?"

Brooke smoothed out her outfit. "Oh yeah, it is."

"Are you and Katie going to do the parade again this summer?"

"Probably ... But that's months away." She saw the look on her mother's face. "I'm meeting her at The Cafe, I'll mention it."

"This year you'd both be queens. It would be fun."

"I'll mention it."

Her mother had been the festival princess and queen, and had forced Brooke into The Festival. Not that she didn't enjoy it. It was the perfect excuse to party; the whole town got involved.

Brooke walked into The Cafe, past Vanessa, and over to Katie who was sitting near the back.

Brooke sat. "She still works here?"

"Apparently so. She'll be pissed you're going on a date with her boyfriend."

"Well, he asked me. And I don't think it's a date." She paused. "Not yet anyway."

Vanessa came over to take their order, a hospitality smile glued to her face.

Katie spoke first. "I'll get a chicken wrap and a side salad."

"Same, I'll keep it simple. And a latte. Thanks Vanessa."

Vanessa scribbled on the pad. "I'll put that through to the kitchen and bring your coffee over."

"So?" Katie started. "What are you two doing this afternoon?"

"I was thinking of taking him over to the hill by Wayton. The spot we went to last night."

"Don't break the tradition of that spot for first timers." Katie winked.

Brooke's eyes widened. "I forgot about that! Oh, I'm definitely taking him there." She bit her lip.

Vanessa put the latte in front of Brooke.

"Thanks V."

Vanessa exhaled. "V. You're the only one who ever called me that."

Brooke gave a genuine smile. "How are things with you, V?"

"Yeah, good lately. Are you both back from University?"

"I am. Brookie dropped out at the beginning of the year. Didn't you hear?"

Brooke defended herself. "The course just wasn't for me. Did the first year and about three weeks of the second, but then decided to come back home and work until I figure out which course I want to spend my time on."

Vanessa relaxed onto one leg until the bell from the kitchen rang, and her body went tight again. "That'll be the wraps."

Katie updated Brooke on her plans for the next term. Brooke brought up The Festival. They laughed, reminiscing, and agreed it might be nice to do it for a final year.

They finished up, paid, and Brooke walked into town to meet Blaine.

He was leaning up against the side of his old Volvo, and lowered his sunglasses as she walked over. "So where's this secret spot then?"

She chucked a can of orange soda to him and cracked open hers. "Towards Wayton please, Driver."

He walked around to the passenger side, opened the door, bowed, and gestured for her to enter. "As you wish, Ma'am."

She giggled.

He turned the ignition on and his Blink-182 CD started playing. The corner of Brooke's lip curled as she screwed up her eyebrows and plugged her music into the AUX. Burak Yeter – Tuesday. He peered over his glasses at her and she returned a look to say, *My rules. Just drive, pretty boy.*

As they left the town, Brooke directed Blaine down the disappearing road until they arrived out of the trees, and onto the top of the hill.

He put on the handbrake and stepped from the car to look out over the entire neighbouring town. "Now this is a good spot."

"I know."

Blaine reached in the car and pulled out the soda, closed the door, and sat on the ground in front of the car, elbows leaning on his knees. Brooke leaned against the bonnet with her legs crossed.

"So, go on then. How'd you discover this spot?" he asked, not taking his eyes off the view.

"It's one of those spots that gets passed down, you know? No one really knows the story of how it got discovered. Many drunken mornings spent looking at this view."

"Let the sunrise wake you and walk home feeling invincible."

"Mmhm. The sunrise over Wayton is one to see for sure!"

"Noted."

The Insider and The Princess started to get acquainted. Brooke spoke about her mother being twelve years younger than her father, and told Blaine about her half-brother Ali, her dad's son, who was thirty-three.

Brooke's father was a lecturer at her mother's university.

They fell in love despite the age difference and had been inseparable since. He had quit his position at the university before stories of their relationship spread.

"I was the product of two very intelligent people making very poor life decisions. At least in society's eyes. But they were both smart enough to know exactly what they were doing, and that it was never a mistake."

"You were born from gossip and rumour. It makes sense now," Blaine smirked.

She tapped him in the back with the sole of her foot. "Funny." Brooke sat in front so they were face to face. "I needed this."

"Another free therapy session?"

She smiled. "A friend who listens, and doesn't judge."

"Those are hard to find."

"Guess I got lucky then, didn't I."

The afternoon air began to cool as the wind picked up on the hill. Brooke asked about where Blaine was from. He pointed into the distance and said, "Walk that way for long enough you'd probably find it." She pried, trying to get him to unwittingly give an answer on his past. But to no avail.

"But, I guess you can't improve without having a past to learn from, right? A way of knowing you are walking towards something better?"

Blaine imitated her smile. "How do you know if it's better, though?"

"I don't know … you just do. You feel happier, I guess?"

"What are you walking towards then?" Blaine lay back.

She plucked at the grass. "Nothing."

"So you're standing still?"

"I suppose."

"Are you happy standing still?"

"Fuck no," Brooke whispered to herself.

"Then why are you standing still?"

"Because I don't know where to go. I studied something that would give me a good career, like I was supposed to, but it didn't feel right." Brooke turned to Blaine as he watched the clouds. "It was all so simple. I was supposed to leave school and do great things … Now look. I'm back in my home town doing nothing with my life."

"You feel everyone's judgement all the time?"

"Except my dad's … I'm just stuck. Because, you know, I stepped off the path. And now I'm wasting my life."

"How? You're twenty-one, you are still figuring it."

Brooke's voice wavered. "Yeah, but I can't be that party girl forever, I need to grow up and move on with life."

"And you will. You need to flow with life. I mean just look at your parents." He sat back up. "Take the opportunities when they come. Until then, relax."

She stood up and pulled that smile back to her face. "You've seen some shit, huh?" Blaine smiled back, saying nothing. "Should we head off?"

He nodded, holding his hand out.

"Oh wait!" Brooke said, as she pulled Blaine to his feet. "The tradition! I nearly forgot."

"There's a tradition?"

"There's a tradition," Brooke repeated as they walked over to the car. "Usually everyone is shit-faced, so it's more normal, but … You need to flash Wayton."

"I'm sorry … I need to what?"

Brooke sighed and rested her chin on the roof. "It started a few years before me. The high school team lost a game to Wayton. Like, a humiliating loss. So, they came up here to drink after, and one of the boys flashed the town and screamed, 'Fuck

Wayton.' The next year they won and absolutely smashed them, so, came up here again to celebrate. One of the cheerleaders knew the story so she flashed the town and screamed 'Fuck Wayton.' Now first-timers have to flash the town and scream it to bring them good luck."

Blaine waited, expecting her to tell him it was a joke. But she didn't. Blaine shook his head.

"Fine, but it's a bad omen not to. You'll be the one with bad luck, not me." Brooke held her hands up in the air.

Taking a deep breath, he smiled. "Fuck it, why not. Who am I to break a tradition?"

Blaine untied his belt. "FUCK WAYTON!"

Brooke belly laughed, admiring his bare ass along with the view of the town. As he buckled his belt, he asked, "Did I do it right?"

"Perfect."

She opened the door for Blaine and bowed, waited for him to sit down, then climbed in over him. He laughed as she squeezed over, kneeing herself in the face and kicking him.

As he started the engine, her music began to play. She unplugged her phone and let Blink-182 play.

He dropped her home just as sunset peaked in colour.

The Kingdom

The first tease of summer morning made its debut in The Kingdom, its eager citizens rising early. The Merchants set up their carts in the streets, The Cooks prepared the day's meals, The Artists bathed in the inspiration of the morning glow, The Royals addressed the court to discuss the month's proceedings, The Insider wandered the streets smiling at The Citizens, The Princess slumbered in her throne room, The Knight mounted his noble steed and set off away from The Kingdom, The Courtesan snuck away from last night's bed and away from The Kingdom as well.

The peace of The Kingdom remained, its pieces still in their correct places, and so the days continued as they always had. The Insider grew closer with The Servant Girl, visiting her each morning as she went about her duties. She began to wonder what life could be for her, other than being The Servant Girl.

As the weeks passed The Insider and The Princess explored the secret and private places of The Kingdom. Stories, laced with lies and rumour, began to spread through the street, so far that they reached The Knight.

The peace of The Kingdom remained, its pieces still in their correct places — for now. But spring was budding its last flower, and with summer nearing, so too was change.

Blaine woke late this particular Sunday morning, exhausted from a week of long hours. He rolled from the blow-up mattress, contemplating if it was time to buy an actual bed.

His position of The Insider was changing to that of The Bartender. The friends here, he trusted, people whose lives he now felt invested in.

A smile grew as he thought of the future.

In the bathroom he admired the latest haircut Vanessa had given him, then shaved and went downstairs as the lunch rush finished.

Jenny offered him a seat outside with her and Sam. An upbeat Vanessa came out to take his order.

After lunch, Blaine went inside to pay. Vanessa was resting over the counter, her chin on her fists, The Cafe empty.

"Good afternoon," she said, perking up. "You were late today. I was wondering if you were about to miss a day?"

"Never."

"Good, you're the highlight of my mornings." She cashed off his tab and pushed the till drawer shut with her waist. "Any plans for today?"

"Brooke and I are going over to Wayton for a change of scenery."

Vanessa fiddled with her ring. "Sounds like fun. Bet it'll be nice for you to get out of town."

"It is definitely the longest I've stayed in one place. But. I have been thinking of something."

"Ooo, what?"

"Going shopping for a bed."

"Is that meant to be some sort of pick-up line?"

"Well, I do need someone to test the springs with. But no," he teased. "I just figured I've been sleeping and blowing that mattress up for too long now. It's about time."

"You probably have very little knowledge of beds. I imagine you're too adjusted to sofas."

"Ouch." He furrowed his brow. "So what are you suggesting? You come with me?"

"I'll clear my schedule! Maybe then we could have a slumber party?"

"Pillow fights and face masks?"

"And ice cream and gossip about cute boys." She grabbed his hands and jumped up and down like an excited puppy.

"I'm in."

"Brilliant, just come pick me up whenever tomorrow."

Brooke sat in her driveway, waiting. Blaine waved to her father who was gardening in the front. Brooke got into the back seat.

"Am I just a taxi to you?"

"Of course not! Bartender, Therapist." She made herself comfortable across the seat. "Listener and Advisor. Not just Taxi Driver. But those are all great qualities for a friend to have."

"At least friend is on that list somewhere."

"Right at the top."

They drove, listening to the radio, Brooke relaxing in the back, enjoying his quiet singing.

Blaine parked the car near the highstreet and they walked through the shopping centre in search of a bar.

Brooke ordered a vodka and cranberry, 3:00 too early to drink it straight. Blaine ordered water, to which she rolled her eyes, saying he was ruining her plan to get him drunk and reveal his secrets.

He shrugged. "I'm driving."

The drinks came and they sat out in the sun watching the people pass, a few recognising Brooke, saying hello.

"Thought we were coming here to get out of the rumours?"

"We are. But I can't escape my fame of last year's Princess title. Even Wayton came over for it."

"When is it?" Blaine asked.

"End of July, beginning of August sort of thing. The date isn't set just yet."

"Are you going to be a Princess again this year?"

"I'm too old. I'd be a Queen this year. Katie and I would have more host responsibilities."

"Do you want to be Queen?"

"Who doesn't want to be Queen?" She smiled.

"You?"

Brooke's smile dropped. "How do you do it?" She sipped her drink.

"Do what?"

"See through my mask? No one besides my father, and now you, can see through it. Who do you think you are? Ay!"

"Because I am you." He saw his own smile reflecting in her eyes.

"No you're not, you've got your shit together."

"Ah, so it would seem."

"More than I do."

"Not really." Blaine slid his drink between his hands. "I lied a little when I told you I didn't run from anything."

"So you did kill a man!"

"No!" he chuckled. "I was like you. Popular, overachiever, and had everyone's attention." He peered at the table. "Still do. I guess some things haunt you forever. But I'd built up such a persona I'd forgotten how to just be me. 'The Lawyer,' that was supposed to be my role in life. My father forced me and my brother into it and I just went with it, despite the fact it was making me miserable."

"What happened?"

"I woke up. Realised I wasn't living my own life. Soo ... I dropped out, my family scolded me and pretty much said it was either I 'get my shit together' and do what he told me to do, or I was on my own."

"So you left?"

"Yep. But I didn't know what to do. I worked a few odd jobs on farms and labouring, things like that for a couple years, just travelling and wandering." Brooke saw him smile as he ran his thumb over The Feather Necklace under his shirt. "I figured out who I was and happiness followed. It was a great journey."

"See, so you did get your shit together."

"For a while, yeah," Blaine sighed, "and it was great. I realised I never got the chance to figure out what I wanted my life to be."

"What did you want your life to be?"

Blaine smiled, his words soft. "Happy. Happy and simple." They both sat, lost in their heads, until Blaine spoke again. "What do you want your life to be?"

"I ... I don't know."

Blaine squeezed her hand. "That is the correct answer."

She looked at him, confused.

"I still don't know where I am going in life, but all I know is I am happy, so I must be heading in the right direction." He let go of her hands and picked up his drink. "You don't need to know what you want just yet. Just be you, and everything else will follow. I promise."

She smiled. "Nice pep talk."

"You don't need to get me drunk. You just have to ignite the right part of my soul and I can't help but let it speak."

Blaine drove them home past the hill, Brooke asking him about his plans for tomorrow, and he explained about the bed shopping with Vanessa.

They both laughed about the implications.

"Are you two getting serious, then?"

"I hope so ... I really like her."

"Then make a move tomorrow! A girl like her isn't going to wait around forever, she'll get other offers. Trust me."

"Thanks for making me feel special," he scoffed. "But yeah, I think I will. Kind of the reason I'm buying a bed."

"Perv!"

"No! I mean because I want to start making a home and stick around! Not for that reason."

"Maybe a little for that reason?"

Blaine's face betrayed him and he started the car. "Home time!"

Brooke burst out with her belly laugh as they drove away.

He got back to the apartment, cooked food, and went to bed on the blow-up mattress, for what would hopefully be the last time.

The Servant Girl

The morning of The Servant Girl's day off began early. She sat up in her bed, swapped her hoodie for a sports bra, slid into her leggings, found her headphones, and went for her morning jog — Album of choice for this morning's run: Adventureland by Reachback, starting song Fairytale.

She jogged past The Basketball Court and further until she was alongside the rail tracks at the edge of town, stopping to catch her breath and admire the sunrise, then she continued back home, showered, and headed downstairs for breakfast, a bowl of cereal with cream and berries. Her mother, Penny, was sitting in the kitchen with a cup of coffee.

"How was the run, Sass?"

"Great! Loving the weather in the morning. Summer's coming so gotta keep fit."

"Are you all booked off at The Cafe for the shoot next week?"

"Yup. In return I just need to be on call to babysit the week after."

"So what's the plan for today?" her mother asked, sipping her tea.

"Bed shopping, for Blaine."

"I'm sorry. What?" A head poked out from the bathroom, the male voice muffled by the toothbrush hanging from the mouth. "And why must you be party to the decision of that man's bed?"

"Sleepovers?" Vanessa tried.

"Oh relax, Gareth. She's a big girl now and he seems like a respectable gentleman."

"Yes, a respectable gentleman who hides his past. I'm sorry but I don't trust him. I've seen him around town with Brooke, and I can see history repeating itself," he called from the bathroom, wiping his face.

"And that's her mistake to make if she chooses," Penny said, leaving the kitchen, cup in hand.

"He's picking me up before lunch so you can meet him and judge him personally, rather than from rumour." Vanessa took her bowl and followed her mother.

Gareth joined them as they sat on the deck in the back garden and leaned against the doorframe.

"I just worry. It's nice to see you getting your confidence back, and I don't want you to be knocked back down." He walked over and sat beside her. "We all know what that group is like. That Brooke Bennett creates trouble for fun."

"*That group* creates trouble for fun. She was just as misled by them as I was."

Gareth pushed his weight onto his feet and started walking back towards the kitchen. "You're right. It's that Danny who's a jerk."

When the doorbell rang at 10:30, Vanessa and Penny were still on the sofa. "SHIT ... um ... pretend I'm nearly ready ... Fuck!"

"Language, Sass!"

"It's English. Don't blame me, blame the dictionary."

"That makes absolutely no sense."

Vanessa stopped on the stairs. "Just open the door before ..." The sound of the hinges and Gareth greeting Blaine interrupted her.

"Fuuuuck," she said softly as she ran up to get ready.

Penny went to the door to greet him too, and invited him into the living room.

"So ... Blaine? Interesting name?" Gareth said, Penny slapping him on the arm.

Blaine laughed as Penny led him to the room. "My mother loved *Casablanca*, but my father hated Rick, so I ended up with Blaine."

"Classic film," Penny smiled.

"Old fashioned, which I think ironically sums me up," Blaine replied.

They sat talking to, or, in Gareth's case, interrogating Blaine while Vanessa got ready. Gareth asked Blaine why he didn't settle somewhere.

"It's not that I don't want to. I've just found it hard in the past to find a reason to stay. Most places don't like to accept change. But ideally I would like to settle. It's exhausting living like I have been, and I really appreciate the life I've stumbled upon here."

Vanessa came down in an emerald-green tight skirt, a cream tank top, cream Converse, and her hair in two plaits. Blaine smiled as he stood up and gave her a one-armed hug. He thanked her parents for the company and went out to his car.

"Pick a single bed, okay," Gareth said as he sulked off upstairs.

"He likes him," Penny whispered. "Have fun, and ... Pick a comfy bed."

"Oh, I'm going to."

Blaine opened the passenger door for Vanessa.

"Your father's intense," Blaine said as Vanessa got into the car and buckled up.

"That's because he's not my father. He and Ma' met when

I was like nine. But he's the only father I've ever known, and because of that, he feels he has to be extra protective."

"What happened to your birth father? If that's not too forward, sorry."

"It's fine. He died when I was two."

"How come you never told me?"

She shook her head as she glared at him. "Really?"

Blaine glanced over at her. "What?"

"How come you never told me, oh, I don't know, anything about you, in general?" Vanessa accused him.

Blaine sucked his teeth. "Fair point."

"Well?" Vanessa asked, turning in her seat to face him.

"Well?"

Nothing, she thought to herself. "So what sort of bed do you want?"

"Big and comfy. All I care about."

"Big and comfy? Got it."

They joked around, looking from kids' beds to bunk beds, laughing at the idea of him in a Princess's bed.

They found a few contenders and eventually settled on a standard king-sized bed. The store offered to deliver and assemble it this afternoon, to which Blaine agreed but said he'd be fine building it if Vanessa wanted to help.

After he paid, the two headed into town to grab a snack before going to the home-ware store to find bedding, again wasting most of their time picking out horrible bright colours until finding a tie-dyed set that Blaine insisted was perfect.

Vanessa picked out some cushions and pillows, ammunition for the pillow fights, and also a cream-coloured set and a bedspread before going to the checkout to pay.

Brooke was working on the register and waved Blaine over. He pushed his cart to her aisle and Vanessa followed, hiding behind him. Eager eyes in the store began to watch as they went about their business.

"Hey dude. How's the bed shopping going?"

"Good, they should be delivering it in the next hour so we are about to head back."

Vanessa blew a loose strand of hair away from her face, head down.

Blaine and Brooke chatted and laughed as she ran the items through.

"Thanks for opening up about that stuff yesterday. Really got me to thinking about my future," Brooke said, scanning the last pillow.

"So does this mean you're gonna be Queen after all?"

Brooke laughed. "Maybe, still not so sure. But V, you should be one of The Princesses this year. I could put in a word? I've seen your modelling photos and you'd be great!"

Vanessa stood with her arms folded, chin in her chest, and half smiled as a response.

"Plus it would be great to party with you again. Still one of the best drinking buddies I've had. Katie can't keep up the way you could," Brooke said.

"I haven't partied in years. Probably the biggest lightweight now." Vanessa's voice was almost inaudible.

"Something to think about V. Would make a nice change."

Brooke bagged up the items and gave one to Vanessa who walked towards the exit. As she pulled out the receipt from the printer, Brooke wrote on it and put it in Blaine's hand as she passed him the other bag.

"Have a fun afternoon. And don't break the bed or you'll be on the blow-up forever." Brooke winked as she said goodbye and served the next customer. Blaine looked at the receipt. "MAKE YOUR MOVE." He chuckled, putting it in his pocket.

Vanessa walked ahead through the car park and Blaine asked, "I didn't realise you two were actually, like, close close?"

Vanessa didn't make eye contact. "Yeah we were, when we were younger. But you know, exams and things and life, just grew apart. I thought she would have told you that, to be honest."

"No, most of the time it's mainly me telling her how I'm the most confident person in the world until I make eye contact with you."

Vanessa carried on walking in front of him. "You two are pretty close now, huh?"

"We are. She reminds me of my little brother. He is annoying as hell, yet still lovable somehow. Has a heart of gold but so easily influenced by the wrong sorts of people."

"Yup. That sounds familiar," Vanessa agreed, distracted by her own thoughts. Then she realised what he had said and turned to face him. "You never talk about your family."

"Huh … I'm letting my guard down, aren't I? Brooke needed some advice so I opened up a little yesterday. Guess I'm getting too comfortable."

She watched Blaine focus on the ground, then up at the sky, his eyes filled with an emotion that the sweetest air could not revitalise. Vanessa relaxed as she took his hand and looked him in the eyes.

"Come on. Let's go fail at building a bed!" she said as her dimples grew, taking Blaine's pain from his mind.

They got into the car and drove back to his apartment, Jack's Mannequin – Lost in Transit playing as they sang along. Blaine unlocked the door, they put the bags in the kitchen, and cleared the blow-up out of the way to make room before the delivery arrived. He made her green tea in The Mug and they sat and chatted about her parents, Blaine picking up some tips to get into Gareth's good books.

When they received the text that the delivery was downstairs, they both went to help carry the box and the mattress up to the apartment.

Mick watched them from The Cafe window, enjoying the free entertainment. He grabbed Dean from the kitchen and they helped bring it all upstairs, giving Dean and Blaine a chance to chat properly for the first time.

Dean elbowed Vanessa on the way out and winked, telling her to have fun. Vanessa was speechless, but she laughed after they'd left, telling Blaine how Dean had been sceptical about him.

"I can't help it. People hate me from afar but fall in love with me once they actually get to know me. I am a book judged by my cover and a story that has been misquoted by someone who didn't take the time to read its deeper message. It's my curse," Blaine said, enjoying his own dramatic monologue.

Vanessa smiled at him and shook her head as she took a sip of the green tea.

"Now ... How do we do this?"

Once they'd assembled the bed, they moved it into place just next to the window.

The pizza ordered, bedding put on, and pillows plumped, Blaine put the old blanket in the wash and deflated the mattress. While he did this, Vanessa made herself comfortable, sprawling across the bed.

After the wash finished, he climbed out one of the windows that led onto a part of the roof above The Cafe, to hang the blanket up to dry. Vanessa heard a knock at the door and jumped up to accept and pay for the pizza. She put the boxes on the kitchen counter and grabbed plates from the kitchen.

He climbed back in and the two sat and ate quietly, Blaine

leaning against the fridge and Vanessa perched on the counter,

She rested her head on his shoulder. "Thank you. I really enjoy days like this with you."

"Me too, they get me out of bed. And now I have an actual bed for them to get me out of." He reached over her lap to put the plate down and pick up a serviette.

"I should also thank Brooke, I guess … for getting you to start opening up."

"Why? You're the reason I'm so comfortable here. I'm the one who should be thanking Brooke for letting me talk to her about you."

"What does she say?"

"She tells me how a girl like you doesn't come around often. And she is right."

"Am I really the reason you settled on this town?"

"Yeah. And I haven't settled on this town. I've found a reason to call it home."

Vanessa blushed. He reached his hand up to the side of her face and gently brought it closer to him, kissing her. As he backed away from the kiss, doubting himself, he felt both of Vanessa's hands touch either side of his face and she pulled him closer. Her hands were greasy from the pizza.

Finally, she thought, letting go and biting her lip.

"That was overdue, wasn't it?" He didn't mind the grease she had left on his cheek.

"Yes it was. But it was worth the wait."

She leaned back in and kissed him again, his hand sliding down from her ribs to her waist. The two locked eyes. Blaine picked up the slice from his plate and took another bite, shutting his eyes. He swallowed and looked at her with a big smile.

"What?" Vanessa giggled.

"The pizza tastes like your lip gloss. I like it."

She laughed and took a bite out of his slice, smiling as she ate it.

After they ate, she cleared up the plates and put them in the sink.

Standing still for a moment, Vanessa spoke. "Brooke was my best friend through high school. We were so close for years, and then when we were fifteen she thought it would be fun for us to join the cheerleaders, so we did. We started getting invited to parties and she started dating Danny, getting sucked into that group. So naturally I followed."

She took a breath.

"But I was still the nerdy book girl and exams were coming up, so I focused on them more than the parties. At one of them I was studying while drinking, so Danny asked if I could help tutor him upstairs. We weren't really close, but he was my best friend's boyfriend so, you know, couldn't really say no. Half way through he started getting … inappropriate. I tore his shirt as I pushed him away. Then Brooke walked in."

She paused to look Blaine in the eyes. "You know how this town is with rumours. The truth didn't matter. Brooke was humiliated and we pretty much haven't spoken since."

Blaine walked over and took her hands.

"I'm glad that you are, but why are you telling me all this?"

"Because you make me happy. A kind of happiness I haven't felt, and confidence I haven't had in years. Everyone has noticed it. I just … I just don't want it to happen again. I'm scared she wants me to be humiliated the same way she was."

"But surely you were just as humiliated as she was?"

"She cared about her reputation more than I did mine. I faded into the background … she stayed in the spotlight. And, by the time the truth overtook the rumour, the damage was done. We were really close as kids. I probably still know her better than

Katie does. She isn't real with them. But today she was real and that's because of you. You're good for her, but more importantly, she's good for you, and I don't want to take that away."

He hugged her and held her tight.

"I am good for you, too, and I promise you," he said, "I will make sure this side of you that has come back, that you are happy about, stays. I promise I will nurture it and help you be the best you that you want to be."

She reached up and kissed him.

"Thank you for coming into my life." Her emerald eyes peered up at him.

Blaine kissed her forehead. "Thank you for letting me in, and giving me a place I can call home."

He looked around his apartment: the coffee table in the centre now that the blow-up mattress had gone, the sofa he slept on that first night now complete with cushions, his kitchen filled with every essential piece of equipment, the curtains over the window able to block the morning sun, his bed covered in pillows, the circular door mat by the front door next to his shoe rack, and The Mug on the counter. It really was his home now.

He dropped Vanessa to her home. They kissed as she climbed out. No Penny peeking through the window.

And Blaine drove away — listening to Overdue by The Get Up Kids.

The Knight & The Courtesan

Before the summer begins, there is a story that happens alongside Ours. A side story, if you will. One of the reasons this tale is one of my favourites is that the smallest nuances give the greatest personality.

But, I mean, it's just a story so it doesn't really matter, right? Well, aren't all our lives just stories in themselves?

And so, I would like you to cast your mind back to the first tease of a summer morning.

Day broke through the window. As she rolled over in bed to see the body lying next to her, she pulled the pillow over her face. The Night before had been long, a lot of dancing, and a lot of drinking.

She stumbled out of bed and straight to the bathroom to pee. Looked in the mirror. A rough, tired face grimaced back, barely visible through half-open eyes.

Same shit every night ... same old shit ... never gets old, she smiled to herself

Closing eyes and stumbling through the room picking up clothes scattered over the floor, getting changed and leaving.

Our Princess's best friend, The Courtesan, got into the driver's seat and rode away from The Kingdom back to her studies.

Actually, no, let's start a little further back.

That morning day broke through the window. As she fell out of bed, she woke The Knight.

He watched her bare ass stumble to the bathroom before he drifted back to sleep.

When he next woke, she was gone. He glanced at the old alarm clock, 9:10, then squinted at his phone screen.

He texted Brooke: why did u leave without wakin me

Dozing back off, he woke again at 10:23. No reply.

Eventually he decided to get out of bed. No shower, straight to the kitchen for food.

The Knight was the middle child of five siblings, his sixteen-year-old twin sisters the only ones still living at home.

He opened the fridge, grabbed three eggs, cracked them into a bowl, whisked them, added milk, sugar, and flour and whisked again.

"Pancakes?" a soft voice said from behind him.

He grumbled a response.

"Tilly! Danny's making pancakes!" Liv shouted, her voice thundering inside his dehydrated, alcohol-damaged head.

"Is Brooke still in bed?" Tilly asked with a mouthful of pancake.

"No. She snuck out at like eight," Liv said, cutting into hers.

"Oh Em Gee! She is so gonna break up with you!"

Danny flipped his pancake, catching half of it in the pan and the other half landing on the stove. "Not that it's any of your business." He threw the splattered mess back into the pan. "But we aren't together."

"Ooo, friends with benefits!" they said in unison.

"Actually we both were laughing about how little action we got," he said.

Tilly took another mouthful. "Bet you she'll end this,

though. A girl doesn't sneak out in the morning unless she's trying to get out of talking. Especially a girl like Brooke."

"And how would you know that, Matilda?"

"We had Brooke as a big sister for years, remember." He couldn't help hearing the truth in her words.

He grabbed his phone.

New Message - Tod: bro lads are meeting at mine at 5 bring a case

He typed his reply: K

After breakfast he studied, napped when the hangover exhaustion took control, then woke, and checked his phone.

No messages.

After showering he dressed: brown chinos, a white button-up shirt with the sleeves rolled two-thirds of the way up his forearm, his hair styled, his face clean shaven. He walked past Liv in the kitchen.

"Forget what Tilly says, you look good. I know Brooke will think so, too."

Danny smiled at his sister and went into his room, grabbed his keys and wallet, and left through the door in his room that led to the garden.

He bought a case of beers and walked to Tod's.

"Danny Boy Bringin' the Booze," chanted Tod as Danny raised the case above his head.

They played a few games of beer pong, sharing conquests, all excited about having the squad back together. One of the guys received a text that some of the girls were already at Mark and Charlie, so the boys cleaned up the garden and headed out.

Danny checked his phone. Still no text.

They greeted the familiar faces behind the bar and pushed tables together to be with the girls.

Eventually Brooke and Katie showed up, and well ... you know what happens next.

Danny stumbled home, around the side of his house, and in through the door to his bedroom. He took his clothes off and climbed straight into bed.

Sent to Brooke: the bed is cold without u ;)

I'll get her back, I always do.

~~~

Day broke through the blinds. As she rolled over in bed to see the man lying next to her, she pulled the pillow over her face. The night before had been long, a lot of dancing, and a lot of drinking.

She reached for her phone and, through burning eyes, unlocked the screen.

The Courtesan sent a message to The Princess.

Message sent: how the fuck did I get home last night?

whats this dudes name?

As The Courtesan lay there, she squinted at the body beside her, trying her hardest to remember what had happened last night.

The last thing she could clearly remember was going up to the bar for the third time and doing three tequila shots, desperately flirting with The Bartender.

Did I suggest a threesome with Brooke? ... Probably.

Her phone buzzed.

She looked the guy up and down again. *I have no idea how big he is,* she giggled to herself. She nudged him to wake him up, batting her eyelashes, pretending to be sleepy, and saying good morning. He rolled over and lent in to kiss her so she gave him her cheek.

"Last night was amazing," Shawty said as he stretched.

"Yeah … I had fun too."

The phone buzzed again. As she read the message, it began to ring.

"Oh shit! It's my dad. Keep quiet." She put it on speaker.

Brooke's father's voice came rumbling out. Shawty paled.

"You have to leave. Like, right now!" she said, pushing him out of the bed and pulling the covers up over herself.

He scrambled to grab his clothes and hopped as he put his trousers on.

"You need to go out the back door and jump over the fence! Quick before he gets back!"

Shawty managed to get on one shoe and his shirt, leaving it unbuttoned. He kissed her on the forehead.

"I'll text you!" He ran out of the bedroom.

Katie jumped out of the bed and watched this poor guy scrabble through the garden, climb the back fence, and fall over the other side.

She chucked on a pair of grey shorts and a red bra and went downstairs to her eighteen-year-old sister, who was home alone as usual. Their mother had left the country with another woman when they were young. Their father was always away for work.

"Who was the boy running shit-scared out your room?"

Katie opened up the fridge to take the milk out. "Fuck knows."

"Did you Jenifer him?"

"Hell yeah!"

Her sister took a spoonful of her breakfast. "Slut."

"Uh … we do not slut shame in this house, do we. I refer to myself as a Courtesan."

"Just a fancy way of saying 'slut' though really, isn't it?"

"Yes, but it has more glamorous connotations." She slammed a cupboard door shut. "Where the fuck is the cereal!"

Her sister slurped her milk. "We're out."

Katie grabbed a banana to throw at her. Her sister put the bowl down on the coffee table, jumped over the back of the sofa, and ran upstairs laughing.

After her coffee date with Brooke, Katie went food shopping, parking the Triumph as close to the supermarket entrance as she could. She filled the basket with salad bits, pasta, cereal, and sweets. On her way out she walked past Tilly and Liv.

"Katie!" Liv called out.

"Hey girls! How've you been?"

"Better than Danny," Tilly laughed, Liv shaking her head.

"He's taking the break-up hard this time then, huh?"

"Says it's different this time," mocked Tilly. "Such a drama queen. He'll mope around for a week then they'll just get back together for make-up sex and he'll be all cocky again." She walked backwards into the store.

"He's in the car." Liv pointed over as she picked up her basket.

Katie put the bags in the Triumph, walked over to Danny, knocked on the window, opened the door, and sat in the passenger seat.

"Hey big guy, need a hug?"

He smiled and shook his head.

"Oh, come on, Dan, you know how this works. You'll be back together by the end of the week."

"You know that's not true, Katie."

Katie sighed. "Yeah, I know. She's not been the same since she dropped out. Like, she tries but her heart's not in it anymore. I think she feels like she has to grow up now."

"Man, Fuck that!" Danny burst out. Softening he said, "I just want her."

"She just wants something new and different. Once she's had that, she'll come back to you."

Danny swallowed. "She is always the one to suggest stupid shit with that glint in her eyes. Since I've been back, I haven't seen it."

"It's Brooke." Katie popped the latch on the door. "The girl let you go years ago. Let her go, too."

"I love her, Katie …"

Katie leaned over and kissed him on the cheek. "She doesn't love you." Shutting the door, she smiled through the passenger window and mouthed, "Let. Her. Go."

That night The Courtesan invited The Knight out for a drink to distract him. They laughed and drank with the group in each bar in town, ending their night in Kestrel, where they danced and drank some more. Katie, to Danny's distaste, had Blaine making them cocktail after cocktail. She'd flirt with The Bartender as Danny stood beside, seething.

After a trip to the dancefloor, they came back to the bar. Katie beckoned Blaine and whispered in his ear their next order. He poured Tequila, Midori Liqueur, Jagermeister, and cranberry juice into the shaker. Making it look presentable in two glasses, Blaine set their drinks on the bar.

Danny felt a warmth in his face as he drank. "Okay, I'll give it you, this is a good one. What is it called?"

"A Homewrecker."

Danny pushed the drink back across the bar and stormed out. Katie chased after him.

"Why the fuck would you do that!" Danny stopped, hearing her heels coming up behind.

"Oh come on. It's funny! Where's your sense of humour?"

"There is something seriously fucking wrong with you."

"Loosen up, Dan!"

Katie took hold of his arm and pulled him back in the direction of Kestrel. He shook her off as she giggled, and Danny continued to walk away.

She stood in the middle of the street and called out, "Get over her! You stopped wanting her all those years ago too, remember! You would come to mine and we talked about it all the time. Months before you tried it with Gretchen!"

Danny slowed his pace and her voice softened. "You tried it with me one night. You only took her back for your fucking image!" Katie cackled. "Well. Look at us now, Danny Boy." She spun around in the empty street. Only two yellow lights were lit. "That image means shit! No one cares, so what was the point? Brooke's figured it out. Things change and we have to accept that."

Her mind wandered off into drunken thought.

"But I'll be fucked if I'm changing who I am. I like who I am! It's fun and I have fun! Sue me!" she said, throwing her arms limply up in the air.

Their eyes met for a second, Danny now calming down.

"Fuck it." Danny exhaled. "You're right. Things have changed and I'm tired of having to keep that Knight in Shining Armour image that clearly isn't me. I'm young ... I shouldn't feel guilty for having fun!"

Day broke through the blinds. As she rolled over in bed to see the man lying next to her, she pulled the pillow over her face. The night before had been long, a lot of dancing, and a lot of drinking.

She stumbled out of bed and straight to the bathroom to

pee. Looked in the mirror. A rough, tired face grimaced back, barely visible through half-open eyes, still.

Same shit every night... same old shit... never gets old, she smiled to herself.

Closing eyes and stumbling through the room picking up clothes scattered over the floor, getting changed and heading out of the back door and around the side of the house.

Our Princess's Best Friend, The Courtesan, left The Knight in her chambers and rode away from The Kingdom.

The Model

The first summer morning of the year. Clear blue sky, the night's chill still in the air, as the sun took its place in the sky and warmed the day.

Our Model sat up in bed, smiled to herself, still blissed from that night last week, hopeful for another. She swapped her hoodie for a sports bra, slid into her leggings, and set out on her morning run. The Model started up and around the block, then past the next few streets, by The Basketball Court, up to the high school to rest by the fountain.

Watching the water as it rippled, she breathed heavily, taking in the day and preparing for the week ahead. The Model had a job in the city, and for the first time, was excited for it.

The shoot was for lingerie, which, when she was first booked for it, felt out of her depth. But now, it was the perfect excuse to explore her new-found beauty and confidence.

Her dimples burst on her face as she looked at her reflection rippling off the water. Then, taking a sip from her water bottle and, watching the deep orange sun glow, she set off back home.

Sweaty and sticky, she went upstairs to shower. While drying herself, she took a moment of humble acceptance, admiring her body in the mirror before wrapping herself in the towel.

On her way out, she went to the kitchen to grab a banana for the walk, and spotted a note on the fridge:

Can't take you to the shoot Wednesday
sorry
Trying to figure out an alternative
I'll text you if I arrange something
Xx

Her heart sank. But she was in too good a mood to let this spoil her morning.

Vanessa arrived at work, walked into the kitchen, and hung her coat as she said hello to Dean. She made and served coffees, teas, and juices, collected croissants and breakfast wraps from the kitchen, and took them out to tables.

The morning sailed by smoothly and midday came around, bringing with it Blaine. He passed her a quick, goofy smile.

"Hello, Sir."

"You're in a good mood."

She swung her hips, a big smile on her face.

"You look beautiful," Blaine said.

"Oh shush." Her dimples, prominent, shone through the hair that flowed in front.

Vanessa took his order to the kitchen, then pulled out the chair to sit opposite him.

"So what has you in such a good mood? Is it the shoot on Wednesday?" he asked.

"Partly, yes. I might have to get the bus to the city super-early, though."

"Partly?"

She leaned on the table with her elbow, resting her chin over her fist, smiling. "Partly that, partly you, partly a new-found motivation for life ... Just feeling good."

Allured, Blaine said, "I can take you?"

"Really?"

"Yeah, of course, I've got the day off. Gives me a chance to spend some time with you, and I'm not used to sitting in one place for this long anymore. It would be good to get out of town."

She scrunched up her face and said quietly, "You are the best!"

"Plus it would be nice to get to see another side of you. You never talk about your modelling."

"Not much to talk about. I stand in front of a camera wearing clothes and they pay me. I only got into it because my auntie is an agent and the money is good."

"Well, it'll be a unique kind of a date."

"Like cutting your hair or buying-slash-building a bed?" she mocked him.

"You count when you cut my hair as a date?"

"I did the first time," she said, stroking the short hairs on the side of his head, checking her latest work. "It was a trial date to see if it would be worth saying yes when you asked me out on a proper one."

He scoffed, "Oh, so you just assumed I would ask you then?"

She looked him in the eye, her emerald iris resonating.

"I see your point." He fell deeper into her gaze and leaned in closer.

The bell in the kitchen rang.

She stood up, keeping him locked on her, teasing him by leaning in closer before darting behind the chair to push it in, batting her eyelids at him.

"That would be your bap, Sir."

Each time she glanced over to Blaine, she saw him admire the world around him.

Today is a good day. Peaceful and happy. Exactly where I need to be. I am excited for the future and I can see something great happening … I have no idea what it will be … I just know.

Blaine finished up, and left for work. She gave him a hug before he went and he squeezed tightly, kissing her forehead.

She embraced him. *Remember this moment, remember how you feel, this moment of pure contentment. What is the word they use in yoga? Santosha! You've earned it.*

The rest of the shift ran smooth. Vanessa locked up just before sunset and started to walk home.

As she passed The Basketball Court, she stopped and decided to sit and gaze at the skyline above the trees.

Her thoughts wandered from Blaine, to a memory of coming down to this court one summer as a teen with Brooke and a large group of friends and all playing basketball.

Vanessa remembered how she had a brief eye for Danny, but Brooke made the first move, and Vanessa forgot she was ever interested in him. In fact, this was probably the only other time since that day the thought occurred. She chuckled to herself out loud, pondering why her mind had decided to recall that moment now.

Her meditations flowed to memories of her and Brooke growing up. Happy memories she'd let slip from her head during all the drama.

It was a simpler time.

Brooke would come round and drag her away from her books and the two would sneak into movies or sleep over at Brooke's, her father let them give him makeovers, laughing and giggling with them.

Then she thought of the time when Brooke started spreading rumours around school, remembering when she burst out crying at work and ran to hide on the stairs that led up to the apartment. Brooke's father was in The Cafe when it happened and sat with her, apologising for Brooke's behaviour, telling her how much he missed seeing her around the house.

"It's Brooke's loss that she has ruined such a wonderful friendship over some guy. She'll realise that eventually, and come to apologise. And when she does, I hope you'll be able to let her back into your life."

He always spoke sense. "Just remember: life is not black or white."

Her train of thought was interrupted by a voice calling from across the road behind her.

"V?"

She turned.

"Why are you sitting in the middle of the court?"

"Just thinking."

"About?"

Vanessa chuckled. "Life."

"Deep."

"You don't know the half of it."

Brooke stood at the edge of the court.

Vanessa's gaze was on the skyline. "Join me?"

"Really?" Brooke stood, brow creased.

"Yeah. Why not?"

Brooke laughed back. "Why not?"

The Servant Girl and The Princess sat. Vanessa's body language changed.

"So, how've you been, BeeBee?"

"… Not too bad … You?" Brooke said.

"The best I think I've ever been," Vanessa admitted. "I hate the fact that it's probably because of a guy … but it's probably because of a guy."

The girls chuckled.

"Yeah … They make you feel great until they make you feel like shit."

"I heard you and Danny split for good this time."

Brooke nodded. "Just grew tired of the same games we've been playing since we were teens. Ya know?"

"He's just a Jerk, really."

"Yes, he is."

"Took you long enough to realise."

Brooke tensed.

Vanessa cracked a smile and laughed. "Eh, better late than never … Fuck that guy."

The two relaxed and sat in silence for a moment before Brooke said, "I know it doesn't mean much now, but I am sorry for all of that."

"It means something for sure," Vanessa smiled. "Doesn't make up for anything, but, it definitely counts."

"I was hurt by him; I took it out on you." Brooke smirked at herself. "I envied you. How you walked away and were fine. I hated that he was more interested in you and that I wasn't good enough anymore …"

"I wasn't fine … Rather than deal with your own insecurities you forced them on to me."

"I'm sorry." Brooke spoke softly. "I'm such a bitch … I'm sorry."

Vanessa turned to face her. "You were a bitch, yes. But, the fact you realise that, genuinely and deeply realise that, means maybe you aren't anymore. The past is the past …"

Brooke joined in.

"As long as we grow from it, we needn't be defined by it."

Vanessa continued, "He is a very wise man."

"He's been through a lot."

A warm smile came over Vanessa, "How is your father?"

"Still the most understanding man in the entire world," Brooke smiled.

"He just gets it … Be kind because you never know what people are going through."

Brooke looked over at Vanessa and the way she sat, confident and grounded, at peace.

"I think he'd tear up if he saw us right now."

"What? Quoting him and not mocking him?" Vanessa gave a suppressed laugh. "I miss your father."

They both turned to watch the sun being held up by the trees.

"I trust Blaine. Not you," said Vanessa.

"Understandable."

"I've seen him flirt. But that's how he talks. It's his mask. You two are very similar that way, which is why you get on so well. He needs you as a friend and I'm not the sort of person to take that away from him because of my insecurities."

Vanessa turned to face Brooke before continuing.

"Don't think I'm comfortable with it … I just trust him. But if you even think of making a move, so help me!"

"He's an incredible guy. To say I'm not jealous of you, the way he looks at you, the way he talks about you, I would be lying. But I see it as karma being paid."

Vanessa cracked a smile. "The irony is not lost on me either."

Brooke got to her feet. "Warning received and appreciated. The past is the past. Believe me, I don't want to relive it either."

"This was long overdue, Brooke."

"It was."

She walked away to the edge of the court then, without stopping and turning, called over, "He's falling for you hard V, so don't fuck this up, Kay. Because if you do … Girl, so help me." And she started to belly laugh.

Vanessa smiled to herself as she shook her head.

~~~

Blaine's car pulled up early Wednesday morning. She came down in leggings and a hoodie. After she opened the car door, they exchanged sweet, sleepy good mornings.

As they drove out of town, Blaine said, "I was expecting you to be wearing something different."

Vanessa took a sip from her bottle. "This is one of the reasons I never feel like I belong at the shoot. I'm very low maintenance. I don't need to look pretty to go and be made to look pretty … I wanna be cosy!"

They spent the journey flicking through albums: starting with Songs About Jane, then to Ocean Avenue, and throwing on N.E.R.D. at the end. Arriving at the studio just before midday, Vanessa went to get changed, leaving Blaine to chat with the crew.

After nearly an hour of loitering around, educating himself on what happens behind the scenes, Blaine decided he would try to sneak into the changing rooms. He went across the street and bought drinks, pretending to be Vanessa's assistant. To his surprise, it worked. As he walked through the room of models wearing various lingerie, he noticed Vanessa sitting in her booth, hair done, wearing a green laced piece, reading a comic.

She caught his reflection in the mirror. Aware of what she was wearing, her eyes widened.

"What are you doing in here?!" she whispered, closing the comic.

"I told them I had gone to get you coffee. You didn't tell me this was lingerie modelling."

"Oopsy, didn't I?" Vanessa took the cup off him. "I don't drink coffee."

"I know. It's hot chocolate."

"Thank you. I can't drink it while wearing the piece but I like it cold anyway."

"You look ..."

Her eyes filled with humour, waiting for him to finish his sentence.

"Are you reading a comic?"

"Yup, of course."

"You are amazing, you know that, right?" Blaine smoldered.

She raised an eyebrow.

"You keep surprising me. Honestly, when we met, you were this shy waitress, with this spark to her. But I would have never predicted this."

"I am a nerd. I like fantasy books and science fiction and adventures. I thought if I modelled, it meant I had to lose that part of me to be the pretty girl. But you made me realise I can have both."

They were interrupted by The Photographer calling the girls to the stage. Vanessa kissed Blaine on the cheek and walked over with the other girls.

Over the next two hours, Vanessa and the other models showed off both the pieces in the fashion line and themselves. Out the corner of her eye, Vanessa saw Blaine's face cheering her on. It relaxed her.

After the shoot Vanessa and the models disappeared back to the dressing room. As she changed back into her hoodie and leggings, she sipped the drink, smiling at its cold coco taste.

One of the girls, Demi, poked her head around and invited

her out for drinks with the rest of The Models, telling her to meet them at a gay bar in the high street called Burly Men.

Outside she told Blaine, so excited the words fell out of her mouth.

"I usually just go straight home after. I am not prepared, but … This could be so good! These girls have contacts and it's so cliquey in this industry, all you need is to have a couple pictures on Instagram together and more private photographers pick you up for jobs!"

"Then we go?"

"We can't just go," she mocked. "I'm in a hoodie and leggings!"

"Then we buy you a dress?"

"I have work in the morning!"

"You don't have to stay out all night. We can leave just before midnight? Message Mick now and let him know the situation."

Vanessa took a deep breath. "You're awesome. How are you so chilled … like, nothing stresses you out, does it?"

Blaine winced. "Not nothing … but situations like this are what I live for. These moments make memories you never forget, all starting with a leap of faith."

"You know, someday you really have to tell me some of those memories you've got from spontaneous living, so I can figure out what has happened to make you so special."

"It's just life." He kissed her on the forehead. "And I shall ensure you do the same right now. So, let's go buy you a dress!"

They walked to the car, Blaine taking her hand.

Vanessa tried on different dresses. "I need to make sure I'm not invisible around all the beautiful models."

"Vanessa, you are also, in fact, one of those beautiful models."

Eventually, she decided on a low-back, champagne coloured mini-dress. Blaine took it to the counter and paid, to which she protested.

"I want to treat you, Vanessa! So just accept it, okay?"

Blaine asked about shoes as well but she shook her head, saying she rocked the casual Converse look. So they headed to an Indian for dinner.

"Thank you for today." Vanessa said as she finished her butter chicken curry.

"It was nice to do something different and spontaneous. Definitely not what I thought I was getting myself into when I offered."

Vanessa giggled. "I thought you'd like the surprise. You must miss moments like this since you moved to town?"

"To be honest, I have had more fun since I moved in. It's been a bit of a mess for the past year."

"How so?"

"I've just been lost, but I've found gravity and purpose again. Appreciating the small things, and days like this are definitely appreciated." Blaine signaled The Waitress for the bill.

Vanessa watched as Blaine gained the attention of the room with his gesture, unaware he had done so, his own attention only on Vanessa.

"It's nice to see you like this."

"Like what?" he asked.

"Not apologetic. Accepting who you are."

"Where is this coming from?"

"Getting to know you the past few months. The Blaine I met seemed nervous about what people thought of him. Now I feel like you are just naturally you."

Blaine smiled, as he said, "It's the same with you. Your confidence today was beautiful."

"It's strange," Vanessa said. "I've been so idle, pondering the future, feeling myself slipping into this meaningless routine of mild acceptance. But now things are slowly gaining momentum. Effortlessly."

As the waitress came with the bill, Vanessa pulled her card out.

Blaine protested. "I am paying for dinner as well. Today is my treat. You've earned it." But her face mimicked a smug five-year-old.

"Nope."

"Fine. We go halves; I ordered a bottle of wine."

"Nope."

Blaine, resigned, admired her as she punched in the numbers.

The Waitress wished them a good evening and they enjoyed the last of the wine — an Argentinian Malbec. Vanessa snuck off to the restroom to change into the dress before they left for Burly Men.

They found the girls in a booth across from the bar and were waved over by Demi. Blaine sat with the group as Vanessa went up to the bar for a drink with Demi.

"You're new, aren't you?" Demi asked.

"Well no, but yes. I've been modelling for a few years, but this was the first time doing anything like this. I don't have the confidence for it."

"Yes you do! It's just like a bikini shoot."

"Never done one."

"Really?! Well you should." Demi glanced back at Blaine who was mid-conversation with the girls. "He is a lucky guy and he knows it. How long have you been together?"

"We haven't really called it official yet but we both are pretty serious."

"If he doesn't claim you soon, I might have to make a move," Demi winked.

They ordered their drinks: more wine.

Vanessa smirked at the floor and admitted to Demi, "I've spent these past few years only meeting bitches in this industry. It's so nice to meet a group like you!"

"We are the revolution. It's about the friends you've got with you that help you grow together. Not making enemies. We like you! So consider this your initiation."

As the night went on and the drinks flowed, they all took a few pictures, adding them to their Instagram and following Vanessa while they did so. Eventually the group ended up on the dancefloor, guys coming up to dance with Blaine, much to the amusement of the group. One guy got too handsy, giving Vanessa an excuse to slide in and intervene.

At some point one of the girls hyped Vanessa up about her shoes and started chanting, "Vans! Vans! Vans!" which stuck for the night.

When they realised the time was now closer to 1:00 than it was to midnight, they said their goodbyes. Demi promised to send Vanessa some information about a bikini shoot in a few weeks.

Blaine walked a buzzed Vanessa to the car. Shortly into the drive, listening to laid-back jazz tracks, Vanessa fell asleep, waking up only to change the music to Jack's Mannequin – The Glass Passenger. Once they were close to town, Vanessa turned the music down and turned to Blaine, a twinkle in her eye.

"So, I was thinking. It's a lot later than we thought it would be. There is a spare uniform in The Cafe. You have that nice big double bed now, and, so conveniently, live directly above my work … Could I stay with you tonight?"

"Makes perfect sense to me."

He took her hand and linked her fingers into his.

They parked and walked up to the apartment. Blaine unlocked the door and they both kicked their shoes off.

"There is a spare toothbrush in the cabinet," Blaine said, filling The Mug and a glass with water.

Vanessa went to the bathroom to change back into just the hoodie and freshen up for bed. Blaine knocked on the door, joined her, and they brushed their teeth together.

They climbed into bed, cuddled, then kissed goodnight, the fresh minty chill on their lips.

"Thank you." She nuzzled her head under his chin, drifting off to sleep.

"Thank you, too."

The Storm

Summer had officially begun. So, it only seemed right for it to be drenched in irony. The forecast warned of a storm.

The Merchants rushed through drizzle to open their shops. The Princess rose early, breathing in that wonderful petrichor, appreciating a long-awaited rain.

The Town felt the change of pressure in the air, although most of The Citizens shrugged it off, thinking it to be the storm.

Talk began of preparations for The Festival. The Mayor began planning meetings with select committee members.

The Model woke after a peaceful slumber, rolling over to see The Bartender still deeply dreaming. She took a sip of water from The Mug, checked the time, and lay there listening to the rain.

When The Bartender started to stir, she kissed his forehead and he opened his eyes before reaching out to pull her in close.

"I slept so good," she whispered to him.

"Me too. It's nice to have someone to squeeze," he mumbled.

The Model's stomach grumbled.

"Do you want a sausage bap before you go to work?"

"What makes you think that? Just because I'm in your bed doesn't mean you can just assume I want it, you know?"

The Bartender rolled his eyes.

"That is very true. I would never assume and, believe me, I'll be a little more romantic when I ask you."

"I would love one," The Model replied, still in his arms.

"A bap or … ?"

"Bap!"

When the morning ended, The Model took her place as The Waitress and Blaine took his as The Bartender, spending the afternoon pouring drinks for passers-by finding shelter from the rain.

This would be the theme of the week as the storm grew darker and the rain grew heavier. Most of The Citizens remained at home and waited for the storm to pass. A few ventured out for supplies.

By Tuesday, The Princess decided she'd had enough of being stuck in and thought it was time to pay The Bartender a visit.

Brooke burst through the doors of Kestrel, the bar empty. Her soaked fringe stuck to her forehead, Brooke cast Blaine a confident, wet smile.

He put down the glass he was polishing, grabbed some clean bar towels, and brought them over to her.

"What are you doing here?"

"I wanted to see you." He handed her a towel to dry her face and together they walked back over to the bar. "Besides we need a catch-up. Haven't spoken to you in weeks. I'm starting to think you might have gotten bored of me?"

"Bored of you?" He pondered the thought. "Doesn't seem possible. Can I get you a drink?"

"Just water, thank you." Brooke jumped up on the bar stool. "So? … what is it like dating a model?"

He looked at her, shocked with how quick the news travelled.

"I saw the pics on Instagram. Looked like a fun night of drinking."

"Yeah, she was a little hung-over the next morning."

"The next morning?" Brooke pursed her lips.

"It was late when we got back and I live right above her work so it made sense for the morning."

"So you watched her model all day and then she stayed in your bed. Damn, no wonder she's got you so caught up."

She twirled the straw in her drink, staring at him with accusing eyes.

"So … did you two?"

"We just slept. We were both tired."

"Bor-ring! Romantic and cute as hell … But boring."

"Sorry to disappoint. I've done my fucking around. I'm happy to have a bit of romance back."

"Ooo, now that's more like it! Tell me more about your hoe phase?" She leaned forward, elbows on the bar, chin cradelled on the back of her fingers.

"Later." Blaine gestured with his eyes over to Tim.

Brooke picked up her glass, frowning.

"Tease."

"So, what is this big summer festival thing then? Tim's been making plans for it all week. I didn't realise it was that big an event."

"Yah! The main event of the year for this town."

"You and Katie doing it?"

"Katie wants to do it. I figure it'll be the perfect punctuation point for the end of a chapter and give me the opportunity to start fresh."

Blaine smiled at her. Everything people had warned him about her was wrong. They all saw The Princess, but he saw The Girl. They branded her and refused to let her change, and she'd done the same to herself.

Tim came and joined them, reminiscing back to the first summer Kestrel opened, when Brooke and her friends tried to get in under age.

She reminded him that they never succeeded, but he gave her credit, telling her they were the most persistent group he'd had in all his years of managing bars.

Tim and Brooke chatted about the upcoming festival and memories from the past few years, Blaine taking in each story.

Turning to Brooke, Tim asked, "Would you want to work here over the summer?"

"I only have experience drinking cocktails, not making them."

"That's fine. It would be great to have one of last year's Princesses and this year's Queen behind the bar during the build-up."

"I mean, yeah, I'm down. Would be great to learn to bartend and would help me save a bit more."

"We could suggest to the committee a VIP booth for The Royals after the parade. With you working here we'd be more likely to get it approved and hyped up during the summer."

"Fuck yeah! Free drinks?" That smile of hers lured Tim in.

"If you'll work on clean-up the next morning?"

Brooke looked back at Blaine.

"I practically live here," Blaine said. "He's already got Amanda and me pencilled in for everything."

"Well, if you are happy to have a very hung-over Brooke, then sure," she admitted, holding her hand out.

"Welcome to the family!" Tim shook and he turned to Blaine. "Something tells me this year's festival is gonna be one for the books!"

As the week went by, the storm worsened. Trees were knocked down and the weather conditions were only expected to become more furious.

Tim had decided it would be better to stay closed Friday night, giving Blaine a night off. Friday was supposed to be the peak of the storm so most places decided not to open. High speed winds, torrential rain, and lightning kept everyone confined to their homes.

Much to Blaine's surprise, there was a banging at his door. He jumped over the back of the sofa and headed straight to the door.

As he opened it, Vanessa flew straight past him, dripping wet.

Déjà vu.

"Our road has been blocked in by a fallen tree and I refuse to walk home in this. Can I stay here until it calms down?"

"Of course! How are you this wet from literally just running around the building and up here?"

She stood, uncomfortable, dripping in the kitchen but there was still humour in her face.

"Yeah, it's pretty bad out there!"

"Clearly!"

He took her coat and told her to go shower, giving her one of his hoodies and a pair of joggers to change into. As she went into the bathroom, he put the kettle on to make her a cup of tea.

She came out, lost in his clothes, and sat with him on the sofa. She rolled up the jogging bottoms.

"I can't believe Mick didn't close today."

"Of course he wouldn't. Sure, he's a nice guy but that dude is obsessed with making money."

"Yeah, but so is Tim and even he closed."

"Tim loves what he does, though, and would always pick 'Good Vibes' over money. Mick is lovely but I've worked with him for long enough to realise he only really cares when he is making money."

"That surprises me."

"Trust me. A few years ago when I started, that place wasn't doing so well and he was a total dick. Maybe it was because they'd just had Sam, but still no excuse." She sipped her tea. "But anyway, like you say, focus on the now and right now I'm just grateful I get to be here with you. I feel safe and content whenever I'm with you." Vanessa cuddled up next to him.

She felt Blaine's body stiffen.

Vanessa looked up at his face, his eyes wavering.

Her smile dropped away. "Too much?"

Blaine said nothing; he just sat staring forward. He didn't look scared or uncomfortable. No, he looked sad, almost sorry.

She watched him choke on his words and then say, "You shouldn't."

Vanessa could see his eyes holding back tears as he avoided looking at her.

Blaine took a deep breath, his voice shaky. "I'm sorry, it's just too similar."

He centred himself and looked her in the eyes.

"You find a way in, Vanessa Gretchen." And he smiled at her as he brought her hand to his lips.

She feigned resistance.

"I told you I dropped out of University and was basically disowned by my family."

"Yeah?"

"That isn't the whole story." Blaine paused, collecting his thoughts. "I dropped because I fell in love."

Vanessa sat up next him, bringing her knees to her chest.

"Her name was Yalena, meaning 'bright shining light.' Damn hippie parents, but it was true for her. She'd spent most of her life travelling and had gone to Uni to study history, but missed the world too much. The way she talked about her life made it sound like paradise. We talked about dropping out and one day she did, so I followed. My father was fuming and told me when it all went to shit not to come crying back. And we left."

A warmth returned to his face, one Vanessa had never seen.

"She was so full of energy. She was wild. We bought this old bus, drove around in that thing for a couple of years, taking odd jobs, working on farms, then packing up and hitting the road and just seeing where life took us. First time in my life I was happy." He began to choke up. "One night, laid in the front of the bus, she turned to me and said the exact same thing ... word for word ..."

Vanessa placed a hand on his knee, feeling him flinch.

"We'd broken down in the middle of nowhere and recovery was going to be hours. Next thing I know I'm in a hospital bed."

Vanessa took hold of his hand and he squeezed back, tight, his eyes blurry and lost. "The truck driver had fallen asleep at the wheel. He'd come off the road and hit us. I woke up in hospital and I was fine. Concussion, busted collar bone, and covered in cuts, that was it. But Yalena ..."

He choked.

"She'd been thrown head first into the dashboard ... And ... and broke ..." He couldn't finish.

Vanessa held him.

Blaine had tried going home after it had happened but his father closed him out, telling Blaine, "You died the day you threw away everything I've given you."

For the next year Blaine fell into a grey blur, living the only life he now knew. As he wandered, Blaine remembered a conversation with Yalena and The Owner of a winery they worked for. Something she had said once before at University as well.

"Life is long! People say it's too short but what they actually mean, is moments. Sure, we could die tomorrow. But if we live each day, fully immersed in each moment, humbled by the knowledge it will come to an end, grateful it happened, we make those memories eternal. Miss those moments sure … but never dwell on them."

Blaine gradually realised he was dishonouring everything he had learned from Yalena. It was time to start a new journey of his own. That was when he found The Kingdom.

The Storm did not ease. But Blaine's mind did.

"The day I met you, your smile sparked something new in me. You were real, honest, you weren't trying to be anything else other than you," he said.

Vanessa hid her dimples behind The Mug.

They laughed through their tears as Blaine poured out more of his past while cooking dinner — sweet and sour pineapple stir-fry.

9:47 - Gareth: Just stay the night and hope that by the morning it will have cleared

Our two sat and ate.

Outside the earth shook, but inside not even a feather would fall.

"Yalena was intelligent and passionate, a complete nutcase and a hazard of a human being. The definition of a wild soul." Blaine chuckled. "But she could so easily let go if she had to."

Vanessa smiled.

"I never knew how she did it. Just let go."

He lay with his head in Vanessa's lap.

"I'm sorry. I keep talking about her. I hope it's not weird."

"Don't be silly! I'm grateful you trust me."

The dishes cleared and everything put away, they curled up on the sofa to watch *Breakfast Club* on Blaine's new television. Towards the end of the film, the part where they all smoke a joint and gather in a group for a heart-to-heart, the power cut out.

Vanessa spoke from the darkness.

"Please tell me you have candles."

Blaine stumbled towards the kitchen, the odd flash of lightning illuminating the way. He took a box of matches from the drawer at the end of the counter and lit some candles before going back to the sofa.

"I really needed tonight." Blaine watched Vanessa, lit up by flickering candlelight. "I just needed someone to know my past."

"I never considered anything like that had happened. You're always so upbeat and positive."

"Yalena taught me that. She taught me 'Just be nice.' You never know what anyone is going through."

"She sounds great."

As they sat, the thunder lessening, Blaine pulled Vanessa in and kissed her.

"I am so happy I found you. I'm sorry I freaked out earlier. It just reminded me how fleeting life can be."

"Find the beauty in the smallest of details," Vanessa added.

"Just like seeing your face light up as you read a comic right before you're about to go show off that sexy ass." Vanessa slapped him on the leg, and they laughed. "I've finally learned to be happy on my own again. But I want to remember what it feels like to have someone else add onto my happiness. But not just anyone: you." He raised his hand and brushed her cheek.

She leaned forward, placing her hands on his thighs, and

kissed him, lifting her hand to his chest and gently pushing him down onto his back. He put one hand on her waist and the other on her lower back.

Their lips danced down to each other's necks. Vanessa took off his shirt and kissed his chest, making her way back up to his lips.

Blaine sat up, his lips still entwined with hers, lifted her up, and carried her over to the bed, lowering her down onto her back.

The storm faded, the candles burned down and out, leaving only moonlight to break through the clouds.

The Girl

The Girl woke for another long day of work. Making her bed, she went downstairs for breakfast, exhausted. The Girl had been used to working all day then going to the bar for the evening; what she wasn't used to was being behind the bar on those evenings.

For the past few weeks this had become her new routine. She was unable to remember the last time she had a moment to herself.

It'll all be worth it. Think of how much you're saving, she reminded herself yet again as she set out for another long Thursday, Friday and Saturday.

The days all blurred together now. Another week began before the other had ended.

That evening at Kestrel, Brooke served a group of dressed-up young girls and watched as they reeled in and released boys all night. The Girl turned to Mel, watching as another guy was released back to his friends, unsuccessful.

"It's really opened my eyes working here."

"That's the fourth wall of the bar for you. We aren't even here in their eyes."

"It's nice. No pressure, no expectations, just pour a drink and disappear again."

"Welcome to the other side, Princess."

Mel lit the white rum in the lime floating atop a Zombie cocktail, sprinkling cinnamon into the flame. It flickered and sparkled, drawing the attention of those around the bar, briefly, before they returned to their conversations.

"I used to watch you a fair bit," Mel admitted. "Out there you seem like a bitch. This pretty girl who got whatever she wanted because of her looks. But I was wrong. You're a really sweet girl, I feel bad for judging you."

Brooke wiped down the bartop. "Oh no, you were right. I was. I got so caught up in that lifestyle, but thankfully its charm wore off. And believe me it's so much harder to get rid of that image than it is to gain it. So it's nice to know you no longer think that."

"Nah, you're alright."

The Girl woke for another long day of work. Making her bed, she went downstairs for breakfast. She left for her first job: stacked shelves, served customers with a smile, stacked more shelves, clocked out, changed in the staff room, and walked to Kestrel.

She and Mel worked the downstairs bar while Blaine and Amanda worked the upstairs.

As usual, the evening involved lots of people in their mid-twenties finding a way to unwind from the nine-to-five, Monday-to-Friday job by drinking, dancing, and socialising.

Brooke ended her shift cleaning the women's toilets after somebody had one too many Sambuca shots … and hated that she could tell it was Sambuca.

The Girl woke after another long day of work. Making her bed, she dragged her body downstairs, poured a bowl of cereal, and sat on the kitchen counter to eat.

"Good Morning, BeeBee." Her father opened the cupboard beside her head.

She grunted a reply.

"You're working hard. I'm proud of you, but you need to

take a break soon, okay? Why don't you take the car on your day off and drive up to see Katie for a couple days?"

"Guess that would be nice. But she'll want to go out and I really can't be fucked," she said, each spoonful more arduous.

"Brooke Bethany Bennette can't be fucked to go out drinking? I should have forced you to get a bar job years ago."

She gave him a sarcastic smile in return.

"Drive down to the coast for a day or something, see where you end up? Take a break from reality and get out of town. It'll do you the world of good to go and refresh somewhere different."

Brooke finished her breakfast, kissed her dad on the cheek, and left for work. The day dragged and she found herself longing for it to be over just so she could get to her next job. She enjoyed working at Kestrel. The girls on the bar were fun to work with, plus seeing Blaine was a perk, even if it was only a passing smile or silly face across the bar.

She arrived at Kestrel and went up to the upstairs bar. It was a beautiful summer afternoon so they had the balcony open.

She hung her bag around the back and joined Blaine and Amanda.

"The three of us on here tonight. Going to be pretty busy," Blaine said, giving her a hug as she flung her arms around him, exhausted.

Amanda peered at him. "Bet busy?"

"Was thinking we should save it for The Festival, but I mean, this might be good practice for you."

Amanda shook her head and whispered, "Prick."

"Bet busy?" Brooke asked.

Amanda served and took payment. "So we started this thing a couple months ago. On busy nights we see who can make the most tips from flirting. Tits Vs Pretty Boy Charm."

"I set the bar at fifty and she hasn't been able to beat it. She's desperate to."

"Oh please, beginner's luck! I've won both the other nights we've done it."

"Yeah but nowhere near that amount."

Amanda whipped him with the bar towel. "Fine, just wait until The Festival. I'm gonna make you cry, boy!"

Brooke smiled at the two of them as they stopped their bickering to go serve customers. It's this sort of banter that made work fun, not a chore, more like it was their lives.

The night ended and Blaine drove Brooke home, talking about arranging something for Vanessa's birthday. Vanessa and Brooke had begun interacting more ... when they were with him. But to Blaine, it was a start.

They had both convinced Vanessa to be one of this year's Princesses, after Demi had dropped her home from a shoot. Blaine and Brooke liked to think it was them, but in reality Demi told Vanessa it is something that would look good for her portfolio.

Brooke said goodnight to Blaine, unlocked the door to the house, and crept upstairs, passing out on the bed. Sunday morning's alarm went off, what felt like five minutes later. Once more she dragged herself downstairs for breakfast, the only relief being that after this lunch shift, the two weeks of non-stop work was over.

Her first full day off would begin.

Brooke powered through the day: stacked shelves, smiled at customers as she scanned their items, made small talk. When 4:00 came around, she bolted out of work straight home to relax.

~~~

Monday morning The Girl woke up, the sun prominent, and she got ready at her own pace, looking out the window at a beautiful summer's day.

Brooke ran downstairs straight to her dad with a big smile and her hands out. He chuckled as he reached into his pocket and handed her his keys.

"LOVE YOU!"

Her mother, sitting in the kitchen, heard her call out as the door closed.

"Where is she going?"

Her father smiled and shrugged.

Brooke drove the Jeep, without expectation, towards the coast. She considered picking up Blaine, to see if he wanted to join, but as she drove past, she saw him inside The Cafe with Vanessa. Appreciating the scene, she drove on.

Rocking out to her music, sunglasses on, Brooke awaited that first dip in the ocean.

She arrived at the coast, parked, and took her stuff down to the beach. Sunbathing with her book, getting up to dip her toes, then she finished a couple of chapters, packed up her stuff, threw it back in the Jeep, and took a walk along the beach.

She came to a spot just below a low, overhanging edge. A group of girls around her age were chilling with a speaker, while some of the guys were jumping off into the water.

Climbing up onto the rocks, she sat with her legs in the water as one of the guys swam over to her.

"Hey."

"Hi." She sloshed the water with her feet, her signature smile forming.

"You're not from around here, are you?"

Brooke took her sunglasses off to reveal her hazel eyes.

"No?"

"It's a pretty small town. I'd remember a pretty face like yours."

"Aren't you the little flirt. So which one of the girls are we trying to make jealous?"

He swam over and climbed up onto the rocks.

"What do you mean?"

"Jumping off a cliff, doing stunts. Then swimming over here to me, glancing back, I'm assuming, at the pretty redhead, to make sure she's watching?"

His jaw fell. "... How?"

"Your game is weak, bro ... you gotta step it up."

He looked over at the boys in the water and then the girls.

"They can't hear," Brooke whispered. "Don't worry. I'll play along."

"... I like you. What's your name?"

Brooke paused for a moment. "Jenifer. You?"

"Tommy."

He took her up and introduced her to the group. Naturally, she fell into the flirty persona, but Brooke wanted to use this opportunity as Jenifer for something new.

She told the girls she was driving up the coast to go and meet her boyfriend, making up a story about the course she was studying. One of the girls in the group explained that they had all graduated last year and came home to work and figure out what came next.

Maybe University isn't the only path I should take, Brooke thought as she listened to their stories.

She befriended the group. It was nice using Jenifer as a break from Brooke, rather than an excuse for Brooke.

Tommy told her about his crush on Abby, the blue-eyed

redhead who sat across from them, and Brooke boasted about her skills as a wingman.

"We flirt a lot," Tommy confided. "But I just can't tell if it's flanter, or if she is into me, ya know?"

"Bro … have you seen the glares she gives me when we chat? I mean, just look right now." Brooke proceeded to fake laugh and touch his arm.

Tommy looked over at Abby who stifled a jealous look before turning back to the girls.

"You are a handsome guy. And that body, dude! If I didn't have a boyfriend, I would soo be flirting properly."

"This isn't you flirting properly?"

"Nope … just flirty banter," she winked. "Trust me, I'd have you wrapped around my finger if I was … I can teach you if you like?"

"Please," Tommy said, unsure if he was intimidated or turned on.

Brooke, or sorry, Jenifer whispered in his ear and he laughed.

"Okay, let's do it," he said out loud.

"Do what?" Abby asked, bringing everyone's focus on Tommy and Jenifer.

"So I've always wanted to go cliff jumping but I've been too scared. When Tommy swam over, he promised he'd do it with me. But I want you girls to join me."

Abby perked up. "I'll do it!" Standing up, the group followed and walked to the edge, Tommy holding Jenifer's hand.

"I can't do it," Brooke said, letting go of his hand, taking a step back. "Someone else go first."

Abby stepped in and took Tommy's hand.

"Let's show her how it's done, Tommy."

"Are you sure?"

Abby squeezed his hand. "Yeah."

"I'll jump with Jenifer after." One of the guys stepped forward and Brooke skipped over to him.

"Okay then. Ready, Abby?" asked Tommy.

She nodded and on the count of three they both jumped, Abby screaming the whole way down. As they surfaced, the group cheered and whistled from above.

Abby brushed her wet hair out of her face and laughed with excitement, jumping on top of Tommy in the water, wrapping her legs around him. He brushed a couple of strands she had missed out of her face and kissed her. She leaned back and looked him in the eyes, shocked, and then leaned back in for another.

Jenifer smiled, grabbed the guy by the hand, winked, and the two of them ran and jumped in. The rest followed in pairs.

Tommy swam over to Jenifer.

"You are good! Best wingman, 10 out of 10, would recommend." And he swam back over to a smiley Abby.

That afternoon came to an end, so Jenifer said goodbye, telling them about The Festival happening at the end of next month.

"You'll love it." Brooke looked at Tommy and Abby, hand in hand.

She walked back to the Jeep, proud of her work today. The towel on the driver's seat, she climbed in, thinking to herself that today still had some good hours left. Brooke held her phone, Katie's number on the screen. Sitting for a moment, she collected her thoughts.

You could have stolen that boy today, but didn't, because you saw the way he looked at her. Sure, it would have been fun that brief moment but … in the long run, he wanted Abby. Today was about figuring out who Brooke is, not who Brooke was.

She opened the navigation on her phone instead.

You've worked hard and are finally changing your bad habits. She thumped the steering wheel.

"Why is it so hard! … Maybe … Maybe I'm not supposed to change…"

No.

She knew exactly where to go. Inputting the address, Brooke started the engine, chilled tunes on, and drove towards The City.

On the edge of the suburbs, as the sunset filled the cityscape with an orange and pink allure, The Girl pulled up in a lane of houses with manicured lawns. Outside the house with a rusted, dinged-up 1982 Ford Cortina tucked in the driveway, Brooke climbed out of the Jeep. Before she could make it to the front door, it swung open, a small child flew out, and clung to her leg.

"Auntie Brooke! I saw you through the window!"

"Hey Beau," she said ruffling the little boy's hair.

His face stared up at her and said, "You're old."

"Jeez, thanks Buddy."

"Beau!" a deep voice called from the corridor. "Come help your mother in the kitchen."

The little boy let go of her leg, giving a cheesy grin before running back inside.

A tall, black-haired man stood in the place of this little guy. Brooke looked up at his freckled face.

"What are you doing here, BeeBee?"

Brooke spoke, nervous. "Can I not come see my big bro?" She opened her arms.

He stepped out of the door. She took a step back.

Raising one of his big arms, he put it around her.

"I'll get Stef to set you a place," Ali said, hugging his little sister tight and bringing her inside.

He walked her into the kitchen where she was, once again, attacked by the bright-eyed boy. Brooke apologised for showing up unannounced after two years of not seeing them.

Stef came over to drag Beau away. "Well, you are always welcome here. How are you and Danny? Still on and off?"

"Actually, I ended it for good."

"About time," remarked Ali.

"Can Auntie Brooke stay for a sleepover?" Beau said as he sat down for dinner — Tacos.

Stef smiled at the grin on his face. "It's a school night but, if Auntie Brooke wants to, and you don't stay up too late, it's okay."

Brooke turned to Beau. "I would love to! We could watch a movie and eat lots of candy."

After dinner Stef dragged Beau away from Brooke and took him to the store. Ali poured two glasses of Cabernet Sauvignon, telling Brooke about his promotion to manager at the car dealership a few months ago, and they sat in the lounge.

"What's up, BeeBee?"

Brooke faked a confused look.

"Oh, come on, Brooke. I might not have seen you for the past few years but you're my little sis, I can tell."

"I'm fine! I just needed a change of scenery, that's all."

Ali glared at her. "Really? Because you seem lost to me."

She sighed.

"Talk to big bro."

"It's just ... I don't know what I am doing with my life!"

"Okay?" His brow creased.

"Everyone is off getting their degree, or starting families, or planning some kind of future. And I'm just stuck working two jobs, saving up for ... Fucking something ... I don't even know! I just feel like a failure."

"Brooke. You're far from a failure."

"How? Like look at our family! You're now a manager for a car dealership and Dad's a lecturer with this respected reputation. And I am here doing fuck all!"

"You're twenty-one ... At your age I was scraping grades on a business degree I hated, wasting my time getting high all the time. You're doing good, BeeBee."

"Doesn't feel like it." Her voice went quiet as she swirled her glass.

"The Brooke I last saw was immature, selfish, always partying, a complete bitch, lazy, de-motivated in anything that wasn't sneaking around, getting into trouble, drinking, stupid boys ..."

She put her glass down on the table. "Great pep talk."

Ali smiled. "She was eighteen! I wouldn't have expected anything less. I mean, I was like that until at least twenty-three, and even after that I didn't start thinking like you are now until I was twenty-five. Yet here she is, still at such a young age, sitting before me, outside of the small town bubble she is The Queen of, worrying about the future."

He sat up and nudged her with his elbow.

"Whoever this new guy in your life is must be a pretty well put together dude."

Brooke stayed silent, as she picked her glass back up and raised it to her lip. "Why does there have to be a guy?"

"Well, for one, your eyes lit up when I just mentioned it. And two, you've been boy motivated since you were five years old."

Brooke scoffed and shook her head. "Oh God, you're right ... He's not even my boyfriend," she groaned.

"Never said he had to be. A close guy friend will keep you grounded."

"Do you remember Vanessa Gretchen?"

"Little blonde you were friends with for years until you were a bitch to her because your ego was too fragile to accept your jock boyfriend was a jerk?"

Brooke spoke through clenched teeth. "Yuh. Well ... This guy is her new boyfriend."

Ali burst out laughing.

"Oh fuck off!" He put his glass down on the table and creased up. "You've got to be fucking kidding me." His laughter extended into a deep belly laugh and Brooke couldn't help but join in.

"Believe me, the irony isn't lost on me either."

"You can't write this shit. Go on, please explain this situation."

Brooke told him about Blaine. How he had inspired her, making Brooke see her life from an outsider's perspective.

"He broke your bubble. Well, by the sounds of things your bubble was already breaking. He was just the catalyst that opened your eyes. Brooke, listen to me. You don't need to try and be a good person. From what I've heard, you're doing a pretty good job of that naturally."

She shrugged the comment off.

"Brooke, just listen! You said you have no idea what you are doing with your life and the secret is … none of us do. Just look at Dad. The guy has two kids by two different women, one of which was his student and nearly cost him his reputation. Out loud that sounds fucking awful!"

Brooke chuckled.

"But that is because that's what society judges as bad; however, I have never seen that. My mother never tried to make him out as a bad guy because that's not who he is. He was this super-intelligent history and philosophy professor who fell in love, and chose his own happiness."

"You make it sound like it was easy for him."

"Of course it wasn't. But in spite of that, he never stopped being a great father to both of us. He had no clue what he was doing."

She finished the rest of her glass in one swig.

"We are all human, Brooke," Ali said, reaching over to pick up the bottle. "We all make mistakes but they don't make us bad people. It's our actions that follow them that define that answer."

Then, finishing his glass, Ali poured the rest into both glasses.

"You see that shit box in our driveway?" he continued. "That was the first car I bought when I was broke as fuck. I have my pick of nice new expensive cars but I keep that because it reminds me, especially around the sort of people I have in my life, I come from a humble family that is blessed with greatness. Something I hope to teach my son is that, the way you chose to live is what gives you the life you'll lead."

Brooke rested her head on Ali's shoulder, closing her eyes and feeling his words.

"I think you've been living someone else's life for too long, Brooke," Ali said. "And you're starting to figure that out. You need time to learn who you are, take some risks, make some mistakes and grow into a life you can be happy in."

A breath fell through Brooke's lips and she took the first sip from a new glass and said, "Look at you, philosophising!"

"I know! I can feel Dad smiling at us from here!"

Ali tapped his glass against hers and drank. "It's a good life, Brooke, whatever hand you are dealt. You just need to figure out how you want to play it and who you want to be. The rest follows."

Brooke hugged her brother, Ali almost spilling his wine as she squeezed him. The sound of the front door opening was followed by tiny feet charging in.

"Look Brooke! Chocolate and ice-cream!" Beau came running in with the bags.

"You little legend! Get over here with those!"

Ali whispered to Brooke, "He looks up to you." He nodded over to Beau who ran out of the room to change into his pajamas. "If you ever feel lost again, just remember, that little guy is your number one fan and knows how great a human being you are."

~~~

Brooke woke up to a grinning face pressed up to her nose. Drowsy, she dragged him onto the sofa for a cuddle.

"I've been practicing my smile like you taught me to!"

"Good! That smile will help you with so many things in life. It's your superpower." Her voice waking up, she said, "But you have to promise me something, okay?"

Beau looked at her, eyes wide.

"You will only use it for good."

"Of course! Like you do," he said, making the grin bigger.

"Yes, like I do. And make sure it is always honest and truthful, because those smiles are the most powerful and most special."

"Can Brooke take me to school?" he asked, sitting on the floor to put on his shoes.

"I would love to!"

"Don't be a stranger, sis. Come by more often if you can, okay?" Ali hugged her in the corridor.

"We'll soon need you to babysit two."

Brooke's jaw dropped into an open-mouthed smile. "No way!"

"Yeah, it's only ten weeks so don't tell Dad yet. We'll come by in a few weeks to give him the news. Unannounced. You've inspired me."

"I won't tell him. See you in a few weeks, Albert."

"I hate my name, you ..." He stopped himself from cursing. "Just take our son to school."

Brooke and Beau sang the whole way. She walked him in and promised she'd see him soon, kissed him on the head, and said, "You're right, by the way. I am old and I'm glad. It means I'm growing."

She drove back down the coast and stopped off at a different beach along the way to sunbathe and take a dip in the ocean before driving back.

As she pulled into the drive, her parents were in the front, gardening.

"Nice break from reality?" her mother asked, getting up and walking over to give her a hug.

"More of a reality check, actually."

"Well deserved, BeeBee. So where did you go?"

"On a journey for my soul."

Her mother groaned. "You sound just like him. I don't need two philosophers in this house," giving a dismissive wave as she returned to her gardening.

Brooke got her bag out of the car and started taking it inside. "I'm ordering takeaway tonight, my treat."

Her father grinned.

"Yes! Mmm, I've been craving a Chinese!"

The Nerd

Sitting on The Basketball Court, watching the world go by, taking in the sunrise while reading a comic book before work, The Nerd meditated over the past year of her life and how much had changed in such a short time. She felt proud of how far she had come and how true to herself she had remained.

She tucked the comic into her bag, got to her feet, and continued on to work.

Vanessa unlocked the doors to The Cafe, counted the till, set all the tables, getting the place ready for the day. Band of choice for this morning — New Found Glory.

She didn't notice Dean enter. He leaned in the doorway, watching her dance and sing along. Feeling like she was being watched, Vanessa spotted him out the corner of her eye and took out an earbud.

"Good morning there, chirpy."

"Mornin'," she grinned.

"You're in a good mood. Is it because it's your birthday tomorrow?"

He pulled out the gift he had hidden behind his back.

She sighed and hopped over to hug him. "You really shouldn't have."

"It's your twenty-first. How could I not? It's just a little something."

She tore off the bow and wrapping, revealing a box with a picture of a bonsai tree. She looked from the box, over to Dean, back at the box, and then back at him.

"For your new apartment!" Dean said. "You know … the one upstairs? Where you've been spending nights?"

Vanessa shook her head, trying to hold back her smile.

"You're not funny."

"Clearly I am." He punched her on the shoulder. "Happy birthday for tomorrow, kid."

Vanessa put the box on the counter and continued to set up, glancing back over at it and smiling. When she flipped the sign from Closed to Open, her day began, starting with takeaways, a few breakfasts, and then by 11:30, her favourite part of the day came.

In walked Blaine.

He gave her a hug and a peck on the lips. With every table served, Vanessa sat opposite Blaine.

"Dean bought me a bonsai tree for my birthday to put in our apartment."

"Our apartment?"

"He thinks he is funny."

"Well, I mean, he kind of is … because he is kind of right."

Blaine pulled out a key ring with a single key and a bow on it.

"You already spend nearly the same amount of time as me there so it kind of makes sense. I'm working late tonight so I thought, rather than give you my key, I might as well just give you your own, that way you can just let yourself in. So … Happy early birthday!"

Vanessa started to tear up. She hugged him tight, repeatedly kissing him on the cheek.

"Thank you! This is so cute!"

"Just made sense, 'tis all."

Blaine ate while she served the other tables, finished up, paid, and left for work, placing a kiss on her forehead on his way out.

An old couple called her over as he left.

Watching him walk past the window, The Woman said, "That's a very special connection you two have, isn't it?"

"Yeah."

Vanessa blushed. Blaine turned back to give her one last smile.

"Yes it is, you are right."

"It's nice to see something real between young people. You have to keep hold of the special ones extra tight, my dear," she said, taking her husband's hand. "Their magic will last forever."

Vanessa fiddled with the key in her apron pocket.

Her husband spoke up. "Even when he does something that makes you mad?"

"I only remember all the times you've made me smile." The Woman stroked the back of her husband's hand with her thumb.

Dean helped Vanessa close, wishing her a Happy Birthday as they left.

Vanessa locked up and walked around the back, up the steps, and tested her new key. She opened up Blaine's apartment and flicked the light on, standing in the doorway for a moment.

Not quite knowing what to do with herself, she walked over to the sofa, noticing a note on the glass coffee table next to a stack of films.

The note read:

> I should get home just after midnight. I
> got you some of your favourite movies
> to keep you entertained til I get back.
> There is a towel in the bathroom for you
> if you want to shower and I've left some

> money in the fruit bowl for you to order
> a takeaway or some shnacks for the
> film (don't go in the fridge plz)
> Enjoy your evening
> Love Blaine XoXoXo

She folded the note up, kissed it, and put it in her bag. She looked at the stack of films. A mix of Sci-Fi, Fantasy, but seeing her favourite film in the pile she knew straight away her choice.

After freshening up she took a walk down to the shops to buy movie snacks, and stopped off at the court on the way back to watch the sunset and finish her comic.

When she got there, a group of young teens were playing basketball. She sat on the bench and watched them play while she read.

They kept giggling and looking at her until one of them called over.

"Hey! My friend thinks you're pretty!"

His friend threw the ball at him, telling him to shut up.

Vanessa laughed and went back to reading.

"Do you have a boyfriend?"

She smiled at herself behind the comic. "Yes. I do."

The boys laughed.

"Are you reading a comic book?"

"Yep."

"But you're too pretty to be a nerd."

She scoffed at the comment. "And what should I be?"

"A model."

"And why can't I be both?" she said, lowering the comic to give them a lecturing eye.

The boys stood silent.

"Don't judge a book by its cover, boys. You'll never get anywhere making assumptions like that, especially when it comes to girls."

"Is that how your boyfriend got you?"

"Okay, well, first of all, he didn't 'get me'," she said as a certain smile crept across her face. "He won my favour. And he certainly didn't shout at me across the street. He told me I was pretty as he looked me in the eye. And a few weeks later he got to watch me model lingerie."

The boy dropped the ball.

His friend stammered before saying, "You're very pretty."

She giggled and stood up. "Thank you. Something to think about, hey boys?"

Tucking the comic into her shopping bag, Vanessa walked away.

She got back to the apartment and ordered food, putting on some music while she waited, relaxing on Blaine's bed.

The doorbell rang and Vanessa grabbed the money from the fruit bowl, opened the door, collected the food, and paid.

She sat on the sofa and watched *Barbarella: Queen of the Galaxy* while she ate her burrito. And this film, really, was her favourite.

After it finished, she could feel herself getting impatient. Vanessa laughed at the irony, and the impatience left.

Taking some tortillas from the cupboard, Vanessa thought, *I should probably stop eating all his food.*

As she sat on the mini balcony Blaine had created outside on the roof, enjoying the warm summer night and star gazing, her phone buzzed

11:42 - Blaine: Amanda and Brooke are covering the close (we aren't too busy) so I'll leave in a sec

Excited, she climbed back in and got changed into

something a little more comfortable, stealing one of Blaine's giant hoodies from his wardrobe.

She watched him park and waved to him from the window. He waved back, locked the car door, and headed upstairs.

Vanessa opened up the door and hugged him before he had the chance to get his footing.

"I could get used to a greeting like that!"

She squeezed him tight. "You're all sweaty and smelly and gross."

"Yeah, sorry, it's humid up in that bar tonight. I feel all sticky."

She winked. "You will do."

"You naughty, naughty."

"What ... I heard of this thing called birthday sex? Thought it was just kind of a given."

"It's not your birthday yet."

"It will be by the time your gross ass gets out the shower." Taking his hand, she walked him inside, shutting the door behind them.

"How's your evening been?" he said, swinging her arm as they walked.

"Wonderful! I can't believe you remembered about *Barbarella*."

"When it comes to classic films, I never forget. That's something my mother gifted me with."

Vanessa smiled at the comment. She knew it was hard for him.

Blaine showered, came out, and collapsed on the bed, pulling a pillow over his face. Vanessa was filling up a bottle in the kitchen.

"Awh, are you tired?"

He replied, his voice muffled by the pillow. "Yeah."

"How tired?"

"Very."

"Oh. Well that's a shame."

He moved the pillow and squinted as he replied. "Why?"

"Well, some companies let you keep the piece you model, and I thought, considering how special a day it was, I would take one to commemorate the investment into my modelling career."

Blaine sat up, looking over to the kitchen. Vanessa took the hoodie off, revealing the green and gold lingerie piece. Then, walking over to the bed, she placed the bottle of water on the bedside table and stood modelling it for him.

"I thought this was supposed to be your birthday?"

Vanessa giggled, sitting on his lap and linking her fingers behind his neck. "Trust me … this is definitely more my treat."

"How?" He put his hands on her waist.

She pouted, "I don't know. Why don't you show me?"

And so he did.

The two lay there, breathing deeply, both with rose cheeks.

"Best birthday ever," Vanessa whispered to Blaine.

"It's barely even started."

She hummed. "I know." Nuzzling her head into his chest, they drifted off.

Blaine whispered "Happy birthday, Beautiful." And she fell asleep in his arms.

~~~

Day crept around the curtains, gently waking Blaine, who rolled over to a slumbering Vanessa, messy hair and drool across her cheek. He smiled, closed his eyes, and carefully pulled her closer as not to wake her, staying there until his bladder got the better of him.

Washing his hands, he caught his reflection's smitten smile. It was a smile he'd missed wearing.

Blaine brushed his teeth and then made his way back to bed. Vanessa stirred as he climbed back under the covers.

"Good morning."

"Happy birthday," Blaine replied, his voice raspy as he kissed her on the shoulder.

She gave a sleepy smile. "Thank you."

Blaine and Vanessa stayed in bed for most of the morning.

Finally, "What's for breakfast?"

Blaine smiled, getting out of bed, and walked over to the fridge.

"A little birdie told me you have a birthday tradition for breakfast."

Vanessa looked at him, anxious, as he opened the refrigerator door. She squealed as he pulled out a cake.

"Cake for breakfast! I haven't done that for years! How did you know?" Grabbing two plates and a knife, Blaine made his way back over to the bed. "It was Brooke, wasn't it?"

"She asked me what I was doing for your birthday and told me you two used to sleep over and have cake for each other's birthday breakfast."

He cut a slice and handed the plate to Vanessa. She raised it up to her nose and took a big breath in, whispering as she exhaled. "No fucking way... chocolate and lime? That girl is earning back a lot of brownie points ... The last time I had chocolate and lime cake for breakfast was probably her fifteenth birthday." Vanessa smiled. "I bought one on the way to school and we ate it leaning against her locker.... Now there's a memory I'd completely forgotten about."

First bite, eyes closed, her smile stretched further across her face as she chewed. Dimples blooming.

Blaine chuckled at the noises she made and cut himself a slice.

"I've never had chocolate and lime before."

Taking another bite, Vanessa replied, covering her mouth. "Oh! I'sh sho goo'!"

She wiped a bit of chocolate from the corner of her mouth and licked it off her finger, watching Blaine as he took his first bite. He licked his lips, pleasantly surprised.

They lay in bed finishing half of the cake before Vanessa put the rest back in the fridge.

"Look in the fridge door," he said

She turned her head and saw the bottle of bubbles and pulled it out, her eyes glowing.

"It's your twenty-first! And, for some reason, we still celebrate that as a significant number. So, what is the tradition for celebration? Champagne! I grabbed a bottle from work a few nights ago."

"Grabbed?"

"Tim's suggestion, so ... ya know."

"Seriously best birthday, thank you!" She skipped over to him with the bottle in hand and threw her arms around him.

"What say we have a couple outside on the roof, hey? I have two flutes in the cupboard." Taking the bottle off her, he handed her one of his hoodies.

After they climbed out the window, Blaine unwrapped the foil and shook the bottle, firing the cork out into the street, and spraying Vanessa — who was stuck between a scream and a laugh, trying to cover her face.

When the stream of champagne stopped, Blaine poured two glasses and hopped back inside to grab a towel but not before she gave him a big hug and made him sticky, too.

They toasted to Vanessa's life so far and to its bright future, sitting on the balcony decorated with a potted fern plant and some upturned milk crates with cushions on top as seats.

Our Nerd, soaked in company and champagne, bathed in every detail of this moment, finishing what was left in the bottle.

She climbed back in to grab a speaker to add music to this moment — playing Platform Fire by Jack's Mannequin.

Penny and Gareth had a BBQ planned, so not to spoil their appetite, Blaine and Vanessa made a bowl of nachos.

Blaine received a text as they walked over to Vanessa's parents.

4:04 - Brooke: wish V a Happy Birthday from me XxX

She's really making an effort just to be nice, Vanessa thought. *That's the Brooke I remember … maybe she's starting to break back through?*

They arrived and let themselves in through the back gate. The smell of food cooking greeted them as they walked into the garden.

Penny came straight over to wish her daughter a happy birthday, then turned to Blaine and gave him a hug. Taking her daughter's hand and asking her about her morning, she walked Vanessa over to her grandparents and her auntie.

Blaine was left with Gareth over at the grill, who handed him a beer. Vanessa called Blaine over, away from the awkward small talk, and introduced him.

More people started to arrive as the afternoon went on. Then some of Penny and Gareth's friends, some neighbours, and Demi showed up with her girlfriend.

Blaine whispered in Vanessa's ear. "You don't have many close friends, do you?"

"I like to keep to myself. You're probably my only friend, to be honest."

"I don't know about that, you and Demi have gotten pretty close."

Vanessa cast an eye over. "Yeah, we have actually. She's bringing a bunch of fashion designers and photographers to The Festival. Yeah, I guess we do get on."

"It's okay to have friends, you know that, right?" Blaine sipped his beer and laughed. "You don't have to be a loner."

"Uh … Says you!"

"Hey! I have lots of friends, thank you very much! I make friends wherever I go," Blaine grinned making Vanessa smile. "But it's not the quantity, it's the quality, and you have the right kind of people around you."

Her smile dropped away as she raised the beer to her lips.

"Brooke doesn't, though. She's only got you. The rest drag her down. They always have and they always will."

"You amaze me." Blaine's voice was gentle as he rested his elbow on the arm of the chair. "Why are you thinking of Brooke?"

"I don't know … just the fact she told you about the cake thing, and that message from her. It reminds me that, honestly, she was the only person I was ever really close to."

Blaine paused to look at the empathy in Vanessa's eyes. "I think she is realising that those aren't the right people. Do you think you could be close again?"

"No." She peered at him. "Maybe … I'm not sure. Life's too short, man, you know? I still don't trust her. But I can see a Brooke I used to trust. Not The Bitch anymore."

"I really think there is a lot you could help her with and a lot she could help you with," Blaine said. "The Festival is coming up, and you two being close for a couple days will be really good for you both."

She finished her drink, tapping the top of the bottle against her teeth.

"Maybe …"

The sun was now fully set. The darkest of blue skies lit up with stars above the garden.

The music blasted — Jack's Mannequin, Vanessa and Blaine singing along together.

Blaine and Gareth agreed to run down to the shop for some more drinks.

With glasses of wine in hand, Vanessa chatted to Demi about the festival and they schemed of ways it could benefit.

The guys walked back from the store, Blaine with a case of beer over one shoulder and carrying a bag with a bottle of wine, rum and cola in the other hand. Gareth carried a case of cider.

"Sass was telling me you bought her *Barbarella* to watch last night?"

"Yeah. She's such a nerd, it's adorable."

"Have you ever watched it?" Gareth asked.

"No, but I probably should, considering she loves it."

"It's so weird. And so dated which makes it hilarious. Never understand how she thinks it's empowering."

"Is that why it's her favourite?"

"Honestly, I'm not sure. The story behind it is that I was watching it late one night, looking after her while Penny was out of town. Well, I say watching it, I'd fallen asleep and it had come on. I woke to Vanessa sitting beside me, fixated on the screen. I thought nothing of it, not knowing what the film was, but then it started getting inappropriate and I panicked. I turned to her, expecting this usually timid eleven-year-old to be appalled, but she was just taking it all in."

Blaine listened, smiling at Gareth's enthusiastic storytelling.

"Anyway, I didn't tell her mother I'd let her watch it. It was our secret. Then she became obsessed with comics, fashion, and pop culture. A few years later, after all the stuff happened at school, she became that timid girl again and lost interest. The film came on one night and I woke her up to watch it. Her face throughout was a picture."

Gareth adjusted his grip on the case.

"I asked her why she loved it so much and she said 'I find it empowering,' which never made sense to me. It's sexist, misogynistic, poor quality, the acting is terrible, and the story is just bizarre."

"Guess that's the thing about interpretation. It's completely relative."

Gareth screwed his nose up. "But its views are so outdated."

"That shows how positive a mindset she has that she can look through all that."

Gareth dismissed Blaine's comment, opening the gate. He walked in first, followed by Blaine, and the ladies all cheered.

As the night came to the end, the guests left.

Vanessa and Blaine thanked Penny and Gareth for the party and wandered home, heads tilted up at the starlit summer sky, as Blaine taught her the stories of the constellations.

The Festival

The Festival week had begun in The Kingdom. Excited, The Citizens started their preparation: some created decorations for the parade, others shopped for beautiful gowns and suits, all continued to go about their duties and services for The Kingdom, the atmosphere electric.

The Merchants at their carts handed out flyers and promotions, The Chefs worked overtime to prepare their delicacies, The Artists thrived designing fineries, The Royals walked among their subjects who rejoiced in their splendour.

The Bartender had his work cut out, ensuring his skills were at their peak and everything was well stocked.

The Girl was exhausted from her duties in the bar, the store, and now her preparations to once again wear the crown.

The Knight had returned a few weeks prior, bragging of his conquests with the other noblemen, watching The Girl from afar, seeing the woman she was becoming since she had left his side.

The Courtesan, enjoying the company of The Knight on occasion, reunited with her friend as they gathered for the festivity rehearsals. The peace of the Kingdom disturbed, pieces of tension scattered.

The Girl grew closer with The Model as they spent time organising events, working alongside the rest of The Royals.

Each morning, The Servant Girl continued to enjoy visits from The Bartender, her days ending at his apartment, relaxing into herself as The Nerd.

The peace of the Kingdom may have been disturbed, but from its pieces a new way of living had begun.

Vanessa woke in her own bed, a novelty these days. She changed into her gym wear and set out for her jog — Six60 the band of choice this morning, starting with Fade to Grey.

Blaine woke a little later than usual, sitting on the end of his bed before making his way into the bathroom. In the mirror he admired the latest haircut from Vanessa as he brushed his teeth and got ready for work.

Brooke rolled the top half of her body off the bed before collapsing on the floor, groaning. Her first day off from both the store and Kestrel in weeks was to be spent doing Festival prep. She ate breakfast downstairs, finishing getting ready as Katie pulled up outside in her father's Triumph.

The conversations between the two were awkward. Katie's topics, as usual, were parties, drinking, and boys. Brooke no longer, as she bluntly put it, cared about those stories, but feared lest her life be perceived as uneventful.

Vanessa met them inside the high school auditorium and the three rehearsed the dance routine with the rest of The Princesses and Princes.

Vanessa giggled at the rhythmically challenged Brooke across the stage.

"So what's the deal with you and Gretchen now?" asked Katie while she and Brooke rehearsed The Queen's routine. "What are you scheming, girl?"

"Nothing ... I don't know if we have become friends again or not. I hang out with Blaine a lot at work and those two are a serious thing now."

Vanessa sat in the back row, comic book in hand as she waited to be called for her routine.

"It's nice to get along with her, and not feel paranoid around him anymore. We can just be friends and it's chill."

"But you're still trying to fuck him, right?"

"No! He's such a great guy and I love how happy she makes him." *Gives me hope*, she thought to herself. Katie looked at her, blank.

Brooke yawned and rubbed her face, Katie watching as Brooke inhaled the morning.

"Yeah, and what's with working yourself to death?"

"I'm saving," Brooke said through her yawn.

"For what?"

"I'm not sure yet. A fresh start or something, I guess? I haven't figured it out yet. Kind of waiting for a sign."

"So are you going back to Uni?"

"I don't think so." Brooke looked over at Vanessa. "I trust my gut. My heart has been pumping at the thought of this weekend. Like something is going to happen. So I've sort of just been rolling with life and waiting to see what happens. Not much longer to wait now."

The group finished up for the day just after lunch, and everyone agreed tomorrow would be the final practice run.

Vanessa and Brooke walked into town to shop for their outfits.

"It's weird how this isn't weird, right?" said Vanessa.

"I know! It feels like we never stopped being friends."

"Well, it's easy being your friend when you're not some bitchy party girl," Vanessa goaded.

"Honestly, I want to be offended, but hanging out with Katie again, I know exactly what you mean. I'm almost embarrassed now, looking back. I really am sorry to everyone for being like that."

Vanessa shrugged. "Don't be, we all have our moments. I think you forget I was, too."

"Oh, you were the worst when we started cheerleading!"

"I might not have been for too long, but I made up for quantity in quality."

"Teen years are weird, man … so many emotions and hormones."

"Adult life is harder though. Blaine was telling me how you are literally working constantly!"

Brooke let out a whine in jest. "I'm so dead! I doubt I'm even going to be any use by Saturday. But he tells me you are out of town once a week modelling. That's so sick!"

"I am. My friend Demi is bringing a group to The Festival: Photographers, Designers, people like that. It's going to be such a great opportunity, so don't completely exhaust yourself, okay? Because I actually really want to party for once. And if I am to get my foot in the door with these guys, I'm going to need some of that Brooke confidence by my side."

"Are you sure? I'm out of practice … I serve the drinks now."

"Oh please, it comes naturally to you. It always has. You owe me at least that." Vanessa nudged her.

"You aren't ever letting it go. Are you?"

"We can laugh about it now … but I'm still going to use it if I have to," Vanessa admitted with a dimple-woven smile.

They walked from shop to shop. Brooke quick to decide on a copper, low-cut gown and white heels. Vanessa, with more consideration, found a suitable peach kimono dress and matching stilettos. Then, after picking accessories, they made their way to Kestrel.

Tim served them. He'd sent Blaine out on an errand a few minutes before, and the girls sat upstairs on the balcony.

"Now this is a strange image … feel like I've just walked into Blaine's dream," Amanda called over from the bar.

Vanessa and Brooke simultaneously replied, "He wishes!"

Turning to look at each other, both burst into a laugh.

"This is really nice … like seriously," said Vanessa. "I haven't gotten close to anyone since, ya know. And now ironically the person I let in first is you."

Brooke winced as she gulped down her vodka. "That's some poetic shit right there."

"Isn't it," Vanessa said with a murmured laugh.

"But yeah … I know what you mean. It's nice to be able to be real with people now and not put on some kind of facade just to fit in. I finally feel relaxed around people. My circle is smaller but I'm happier."

"Tim was right!" Blaine called as he climbed the stairs. "He says to me, 'Mate go upstairs … you'll not even believe it when you see it,' and he's right … this is weird …"

"Good weird?" asked Vanessa.

"Very good weird."

The three chatted before Blaine took their second order of drinks and returned to work.

The girls sat laughing and drinking for the next hour until Mel showed up and Blaine clocked out. They walked out to Blaine's car, Brooke calling shotgun when she was in view.

"I mean that doesn't count," Vanessa argued. "I have girlfriend privileges, surely."

They both looked to Blaine.

"Sorry Vans but the rules of shotgun clearly say, whoever calls when in eyeshot of the vehicle claims the front seat and command of the music."

"Traitor …"

Brooke boasted, jumping into the passenger side and plugging in her phone — Jon Bellion: Translation Through Speakers, starting song For The Dreamers.

Vanessa and her singing along together, Blaine cruising,

grateful for the discovery of new music. He dropped Brooke home and she went straight upstairs to relax, falling asleep ten minutes after walking through the door. Her father woke her for dinner; after she ate, she headed straight back to bed.

Blaine and Vanessa drove to the supermarket to pick up ingredients and went back to his apartment — cooking up a lasagne with dough balls and garlic butter. They also relaxed for a bit before both getting an early night.

It was going to be a long weekend.

The Jerk and The Bitch

Welcome back to the side story. With The Festival a couple days away, let's do a little time hop again.

As summer became clear, Our Knight and Courtesan made their way back to The Kingdom. Danny had thrown himself into his studies, trying his hardest to move on. Katie … Well, Katie continued to do what she loved. Party and enjoy her youth.

The end of the second week home, The Knight left his chamber just before midday, and like always on mornings when he felt low, made pancakes.

He plated up the first one only to have it stolen out from him by Tilly.

"Yay! Your pancakes are the best, Dan."

"Wouldn't know, apparently I don't get to eat them."

She smiled at him as she took a bite, her face relaxing in enjoyment.

With a mouthful she said, "Can you ge' me a few bo'les of wine for tonigh'?" She swallowed. "Our parents refused to buy me some in an attempt to stop me from throwing a party while they are away."

"They don't want you having a party … and you want me to just disrespect that?"

"Oh come on, you had the other two to buy you beer when they went out of town."

"Yeah, but I'd have like ten people, not a whole party."

She batted her eyelashes and gave a flirty smile. "Pretty please?"

He plated up the next pancake for himself.

"Okay … but I'm going out with the boys. When Mark and Charlie closes, we are coming back here and whatever is left in the house is fair game."

"Yay! Deal, I'll get some of the guys who are coming to bring some cases. They are lightweights, so there'll be loads spare."

She took another mouthful of pancakes.

Danny nodded in approval of the idea of stealing beers from teens. It was a rite of passage: the circle of life.

Liv walked in half asleep, picked up the plate Danny had just made, and sat next to Tilly, drenching the pancakes in lemon juice.

Danny stared at her.

"Really …"

Liv took a big bite and spoke sleepily with her mouth full. "Sho' Goo'!"

Tilly also spoke with a mouthful of pancakes. "Dan's buyin' ush wine for tonigh'."

"Shwee'." Liv attempted to articulate as she chewed.

That night while in Mark and Charlie, Danny found out from Tod that Brooke had been working in Kestrel, so they all agreed to head over and see what the talent was like.

They found Katie with some other friends in a booth near the door. Danny's gaze drifted towards the bar as he watched Brooke and Blaine interact. His stomach burned as she laughed that deep belly laugh at Blaine.

"You not over that yet, Dan?"

Katie slid in, blocking the view of the bar, and kissed his cheek.

"I thought I was."

"Well, let's not go throwing drinks tonight," she winked.

The group rotated from the booth, to the bar, to the dancefloor, and then back to the booth for most of the night.

Katie danced with guys, getting them excited before returning to Danny or Tod, leaving a trail of keen eyes and disheartened souls on the dancefloor.

Danny had tried to order drinks from Brooke, but each time was intercepted by Mel or Blaine, as Brooke snuck away.

After a few attempts, a frustrated Danny was led outside by Tod, Katie, and two of the girls. They stood in the mild summer night air, now past their peak of intoxication and merely tipsy. One of the girls pulled out a packet of cigarettes and Tod, a social smoker, accepted when she offered him one.

Danny's head heavy, he stared at the ground while the others chatted.

Katie once again slid in next to him, lifting his arm and putting it around her shoulder, resting her head into his neck.

Her voice was sympathetic. "You all good, buddy?"

"Yeah … just a little drunk so emotions are high, you know?"

"What say we grab some drinks and head back somewhere?"

Tod pitched in, exhaling smoke, "Yeah, it's dead in there, anyway."

"My sisters are having that party tonight back at mine. Chill in my room and steal the booze I bought them?"

"Stealing booze off teens?" Tod paused as he took his final drag. "Oh, how the tables have turned. My time has come! The power exchange feels good!"

He patted Danny on the back and linked arms with the girls as he strode, leading the way. Danny watched his friend.

It does feel good, he thought admiring his friend's ego.

Katie took his arm.

"I think that's the first honest smile I've seen you make tonight." And she dragged him off the wall to follow Tod.

As the five walked up the path to Danny's front door, they could feel the bass of the music. They walked past a young guy throwing up at the edge of the garden, Tod laughing at the boy and Danny reminding Tod that it used to be him. The house was reasonably tidy, as tidy as a house can be during a teen house party. The kids barely even noticed the group of early-twenties walk in, until a very tipsy Liv saw her brother.

"Dannyyyy," she said, throwing her arms around him. "I'm. I'm a li'l dr-unk."

He chuckled at his little sister and squeezed her tight.

"Where's Til?"

"In her room."

Danny raised his eyebrows.

"Oh shit … She's gonna kill me."

Danny walked down the corridor to his sister's room, marked with a bra, and raised his hand to bang on the door.

Katie grabbed his shoulder. "Can I do it?" she smiled at him.

He shook his head and thumped on the door, pushing it ajar. Danny didn't look in, but Katie did, seeing Tilly in bed with a girl and a nervous boy.

"Out," Danny's voice enunciated, stern but calm.

The girl wrapped herself in a blanket and sulked under his arm, which was holding the door open, grabbing her bra off the door handle, and ran across into the bathroom. The boy fumbled, pulling his underwear up, picking his clothes and the girl's clothes off the floor, and scurried across to join her in the bathroom.

"You're such a JERK!" Tilly shouted, pulling the covers over her face and sinking into the bed.

"Get dressed, Matilda. I bought you drinks … but this is just taking the piss now. You've got some dude throwing up outside to deal with." He pulled the door closed, saying, "Welcome to the world of the host."

"You're sexy when you're being tough." Katie nudged him in the ribs and went to join the others in the kitchen.

Tod had grabbed an untouched six-pack from the fridge, and the girls had a full bottle of cheap wine, half a bottle of cheap sparkling, and a stack of washed red solo cups. Cracking open one of the beers, Tod handed it to Danny.

As Danny took a sip, Tod looked at him with a boyish grin and said, "Power exchange feeling good?"

Danny shook his head but allowed a brief smile.

The five went and sat in Danny's room, reminiscing about old house parties they had been to when they were teens, and decided to play some drinking games in honour of that. Katie and Danny moved closer to each other as the games went on, until she lay with her head in his lap.

Gradually the music outside died down and the voices disappeared. They finished what was left of the wine and Tod passed out on the floor next to the bed. The girls stripped down to their underwear and climbed into Danny's bed while he left the room to grab some pillows and blankets.

Tilly was skulking as she tidied and avoided eye contact as he came out. Liv, who had spent the majority of the party keeping the house clean, was in the living room with a few people that had decided to stay the night, finishing up their drinks.

Danny grabbed two shot glasses and filled them with tequila, putting one down in front of Tilly. She looked at him confused, so he raised his.

"You can't just disappear as the host. That's how the house gets trashed and you get stopped from having fun for the next few months. I wasn't mad at you, I just want to make sure you don't make the same mistakes I did."

She picked up the glass and touched it to his in the air. Tilly winced and chased the shot with a cider left on the counter, and he put his arm around her, squeezing her close.

"Go enjoy the rest of the night, Til. I'll help you clean up in the morning."

He returned to his room, throwing a blanket on Tod, who woke up, thanked him, and rolled over back to sleep.

As Danny made himself as comfortable as he could on the floor, Katie rolled out of the bed to lie beside him, pulling the blanket over her body and cuddling in close.

The morning came and went, Tod and the two girls leaving with it. Danny crawled up into his own bed and drifted back off to sleep while Katie walked down the corridor to the bathroom.

She looked at herself in the mirror, smiling through her smudged make-up, and went to the kitchen. Searching the cupboards, she found a box of couscous, then grabbed some peppers and an onion from the fridge.

Katie chopped up the vegetables and threw everything in a pan to fry. The smell woke up those who were left in the house, Tilly coming out of her room and into the kitchen to sit at the counter.

"Morning." Tilly squinted through hung-over eyes.

"Morning Sista! Nice work last night!" Katie winked. "I'm proud of you."

"Danny isn't."

"He's your big brother. He isn't supposed to be proud of that stuff. He is just looking out for you. But don't think for a second what you did was wrong. It's all fun and games, and your brother has played his, believe me. He just wants to make sure you stay safe."

136

Tilly slumped onto the counter. "He didn't have to be such a jerk, though."

"It's new to him. He doesn't know the right way to deal or process it yet. Brooke told me about the time your sister Kim walked in on them one time. She screamed at him. At least he was calm about it with you," she said, as she stirred the pan.

"He made me feel like a … I don't know … a slut."

Katie tutted. "You are not a slut. You are just curious and nothing is wrong with that. It is better to do it now … I had a threesome with these guys a few months ago. They are a couple now! Neither realised they were gay. Now that was a fun night!"

Katie smiled, pointing the spoon at Tilly, who giggled.

"That's why I call myself a courtesan! I provide an experience for everyone where they can feel safe and enjoy themselves guilt-free. People don't understand it. It isn't being a 'Slut.' It's just having fun, being safe, and living a life that makes you happy because it makes you feel good!"

"Getting a bit preachy there," Tilly pouted back. "But I know what you mean. Yeah … just need to be safe and smart about it. Fuck people's opinions when it doesn't concern them."

"Exactly! Sorry. I'm just used to justifying it constantly."

Tilly curled her lips. "Scared to explain it to Brooke?"

Katie's eyes widened. "No, Brooke gets why I like to do what I do."

"But she won't get why you slept with Danny?"

"We didn't sleep together …"

"Not last night. But you did a couple nights ago." Katie looked at her, stunned. "You have to sneak past my window to get round to the gate."

Katie took the pan off the heat and portioned it into two bowls, grabbing two forks out of the drawer and giving Tilly a bowl, her face heavy.

"That's the only time I've ever felt guilty."

"Because that's a Bitch move," Tilly said, reaching for the bowl.

Katie pulled it away, Tilly raising her hands to surrender.

"Don't hate me for saying the words already in your head."

Katie paused, looking at her, and slowly pushed it back towards her.

"He's just so hot!"

Tilly was about to take a mouthful of the couscous. "Dude, that's my brother!"

"Anyway, it's not like we are even close anymore. She's ignored me since I came back. She thinks she's all grown up but I know she's just getting close to that Bartender so she can get back at Vanessa. She's got everyone fooled, thinking she's 'getting her life together' …"

Katie hopped up on the counter, contemplating. "Actually, I'm kind of proud of her for being that good of an actress! I'm the only one who knows her properly, though. She's cunning and evil."

"Maybe distancing you is part of her plan to make it more convincing?"

"Maybe … in that case she doesn't need to know about that night. And until then I have a broken boy's heart to fix. It's my duty to help any way I can."

Tilly picked up her bowl and made her exit. "I don't want to hear about it … or even hear it when it happens. But thanks for breakfast and the advice! Much love!"

"It's above average!" she called as Tilly left, hearing a grotesque moan flow through the corridor, and Katie chuckled on her own as she ate her couscous.

As the weeks went on, Katie spent nights with Danny. Some in his room, others at her house. The two embraced each other's company; it began to feel natural. Two friends having fun.

The Festival looming, Katie had been seeing a lot more of Brooke, watching her grow close with Vanessa.

Is this still a game? Of course it is. Brooke will ruin this girl in front of the whole town and then she'll laugh about it with me at the after-party. It was the only thing Katie could think of.

So, until that after-party, Katie continued to have her fun with Danny, spending a night with him and picking Brooke up the next morning. Once he and Brooke got back together, the liaison would become a fun little secret between them, they both imagined.

But they didn't count on other eyes watching the secret lovers.

The Bartender

Saturday morning woke The Bartender. Rolling over to hug the body beside him and feeling nobody there, he remembered she'd spent the night in her own bed.

He rubbed his eyes and mentally prepared for the day. From his window he could already hear voices in the street. He peered through the curtain. The streets were packed, cars parked all along the roads.

This small town overflowed, people spilling out of every corner, carefree as they wandered. He looked at the clock that was now hung by the door: 9:27. The Bartender went into the bathroom, used the toilet, brushed his teeth, threw on some shorts and a hoodie, and then, taking The Feather Necklace from the lamp, he went downstairs to The Cafe.

~~~

Last night's shift had been very quiet, not what he thought the first day of The Festival weekend would be.

"Argh, that's the calm before the storm, me boy!" reassured Tim in his worst pirate voice. Mel and Amanda's unimpressed faces dissuading him, he continued, "People tend to come here for a few and plan out tomorrow. But trust me, I am going to need you here at 1:00. After lunch is when the day of drinking begins."

Tim was right. Just after midnight most people had called it a night. On his way out he said, "I might need you to be a bit of a bouncer from behind the bar tomorrow."

"Sure thing, Cap'n." Blaine saluted as he wiped down the bar.

"Cheers, B. Really glad you stuck around here. You're part of the family now. You'll see tomorrow that it was worth staying."

Tim pointed to one of the promotional posters around the bar. They featured Brooke behind the bar, saying, "The Royal After-Party, because even The Queen has to let her hair down."

"I'm gonna stick you on the outside bar so you can watch the parade. That way you get some enjoyment before Brookie drags an army through our gates." Tim chucked his jacket over his shoulder and wished the two a good night's rest.

Mel filled Blaine in on past years' antics. She told him the story that five years ago there had been a bar that got shut down because it was serving minors — unknowingly, of course. She warned him of the tradition for kids who have finished high school to use this as a final hurrah. She assured him they usually gave up and went to The Hill to drink.

~~~

As The Bartender came down the stairs from the apartment and around the corner, he was already walking through crowds of people. The outside of The Cafe was fully seated; some people were leaning against the walls between the windows. He walked in the fully-seated restaurant to find Vanessa and Jenny overwhelmed. An unfamiliar man behind the counter serving takeaway orders and brewing coffee smiled over to Blaine.

Vanessa finished taking an order, giving a service smile as she walked away, which changed to a smile of relief as she noticed Blaine. She rushed towards him, rising onto tiptoes, pecking his cheek, before continuing on to the kitchen.

Jenny grinned when she came over.

"Do you need a hand?" Blaine asked.

"You're an angel! Can you run those over to table six?" Jenny pointed to the tray of drinks on the front counter.

Blaine, fully equipped with his bed head, baggy jumper, peach shorts, and Espadrille shoes, picked up the tray and served the table. For the next hour he helped to clear tables and run drinks, popping into the kitchen to help wash up for Mick and Dean.

Blaine and Dean had great chemistry and both agreeing how well they got on and said they should hang out more, before Mick stopped their chat.

By 11:00, The Cafe was calming down. The excited citizens had begun to make their way towards the town centre, ready for the festivities to begin.

"Cheers for the help, man," Dean thanked Blaine.

"I don't really know how I managed to get involved, to be fair." Blaine dried his hands after finishing washing up the last of the plates.

"Because you're a true gentleman," said Jenny who had come through the door. "A Prince who makes his lady's life easier, however he can."

"Wait 'til the honeymoon phase is over," Mick pitched in.

Dean laughed, "Cynical bastard."

Mick continued. "But seriously, thank you. I know I can be a dick when I'm stressed ..."

"Just when you're stressed?" Jenny and Dean both muttered under their breath.

"... but you really helped out a lot. Take your pick off the menu. It's on the house."

"Yeah man, what do you want? I'll get it started right now." Dean grinned.

"Sausage roll? I should probably eat something good to set me up ... I think it's hit me how long today is going to be."

"I'll make it three," Dean winked, Mick now talking with the man behind the counter. "You can eat one here and I'll make you a couple for the road."

"Legend!"

Vanessa came bursting through the door and into the kitchen, throwing her arms around Blaine and smashing her lips into his.

"You, my friend, are an absolute hero!" They locked eyes. "I'm stickier than the other night. Can I use your shower quick? I have to get into town in the next hour." Blaine shook his head with a smile of disgust.

"T ... M ... I!" said Dean, standing by the grill.

Vanessa's eyes widened. "I forgot you were in here ..."

"Cheers."

"I meant because I'm sweaty ..." She scrambled.

Blaine put his face in his hands and laughed. "Just stop talking!"

She stood there, awkward. Dean shook his head at her while he cut the bread. Blaine then told her to go and shower before she was late. Vanessa gave him a peck on the lips and ran back out of the door, waving goodbye to Jenny, Mick, and The Man behind the counter.

"Who is that guy?" Blaine asked.

"My boyfriend," Dean said with a smug smile. "Yeah, you're not the only one who came to the rescue today ... but I mean he's getting paid in money, not food." Dean handed Blaine the first sausage roll.

Blaine closed his eyes to embrace the aroma.

The sun now just past its peak in the clear summer sky, Our Bartender took his place behind the bar, under the gazebo that was set up next to the parade path, just down from the main stage.

Our Nerd, Our Girl, and Our Courtesan dressed in their fine attires, Our Knight and his sisters strolled amongst the crowd, along with all the other familiar citizens from far and wide.

And so, The Mayor took to the stage, welcoming everyone, followed by The Queens and Kings. Introductions were made, announcements of joy decreed, and the parade began.

Entering first, the performers from the high school: Cheerleaders, Band Members, Honorary Students, and Teachers, followed by the Emergency Service Teams. It was the perfect opportunity for The Citizens to show their gratitude.

Amanda, Blaine and Mel were running the outsider bar. It was a simple set up: two kegs, a cooler of beers and cider, another filled with soft drinks, and another with water. Business was fast already, just as it had been at The Cafe.

Blaine had done a stock run back to Kestrel for cases of ciders and soft drinks. Tim floated between the bar and the gazebo, bringing odd stock on each trip. He was helping Blaine on a second run for a keg and, as they tapped it, Blaine watched Amanda accept a tip.

"Damn, I'm on fire!" she said, helping them shuffle the keg into place.

"Only because I'm busy running back and forth for stock."

"Excuses, excuses, B. Just scared you'll lose?"

Blaine looked at her with determination. "Oh, we're playing it that way today?"

"Gloves are off, my friend. Today is the big day, after all."

With burning rivalry, they both jumped back to the bar to serve. A glow lingered in the service smiles drawn across their faces.

The Band took to the music pit in front of the stage and played as more floats and groups from small businesses walked the parade. Some of the newer businesses had small stands in the street, selling and promoting, just as they would at the markets, now to a larger audience.

The other bars had refreshment stands set up around the street, some closer to the parade route. Kestrel's advertising was superior, though. The sign hanging from the gazebo said: "KESTREL: Queen's Choice." As Tim says, "Tacky works! I don't get why people are so defensive about it. Same reason people go nuts for cheesy classics. I've gotta use it, if anything, purely for the irony."

The crowds cheered as the first parade walk came to an end, The Band playing on as the floats dispersed.

"So I'm still confused by this whole thing," Blaine said as he and Tim loaded up the next dolly of stock back at Kestrel. "What is it about?"

Tim stacked some cases from the stock room.

"What do you mean?"

"What's the point?"

"Morale, kinda." Tim stopped to think. "I guess a sense of purpose and belonging, something to look forward to? I don't really know if there is one way to explain it. It's personal. Depends who you ask."

He put the final case on the top of the stack before continuing.

"It's been happening since I was a kid, but back then it was just a bit of fun and entertainment. Still is, I guess. It's a chance to break away from normal everyday life that starts to feel menial." Tim kicked his dolly onto its wheels and pushed it around the front of the bar. "I mean, even though we are working, you can just feel the atmosphere, can't you? People are happy just to be here."

"Yeah, it's great to be a part of." Blaine was hoping for a definite answer but he understood what Tim meant.

"If you ask me, we complicate life too much. This day lets people breathe and have some fun and at the same time, it's helping businesses to grow. It's just an all-round positive thing for The Town and its people, so each year it gets bigger and better."

"But the whole theme with the Princesses and Princes stuff? What's that about?"

Tim let out a burst of laughter. "Great ego boost for those involved! A day they can feel like they are better than they are every other day of their dull lives."

"That's kind of a cynical view, isn't it?"

"What, nah, it's true! But for some people it's enough and I say, fair play to them, let them enjoy it. Deep down even they know that's all it is, but they still focus on the materialistic things, wondering why they hate the lives they lead."

"So you are saying, live in the moment? Don't dwell on it too much?"

"Exactly! It's a celebration! They forget about the day-to-day, and for a brief moment, are provided this … thing … a memory. A symbol that life is great. And that is what makes it all worth it."

They wheeled the dollies through the crowds and Tim smiled. "By the end of this, you'll understand. You'll find something that'll stick with you and always remind you to be happy, just because it happened."

Blaine sensed The Feather Necklace against his chest. "I guess sometimes we do over-complicate it and think too deeply. If it works and it makes you happy, just embrace it, don't question it."

"Now you're getting it."

As they unloaded the beers into the cooler and stowed the extra bottles of water under the table, the sound of Brooke's voice came from the speakers by the stage.

Tim gasped.

"B, I'll cover you for a moment. Take a break and go watch. You won't wanna miss this! It's been my favourite part since I was a kid."

Amanda called over as Blaine walked away. "More tips for me? You're making this too easy!"

"I'm giving you a head start so that it's more fair," he shouted back.

Amanda scoffed at his arrogance but it made her smile.

Blaine made his way through the crowds as Brooke and Katie talked over the sound system, announcing this year's Princesses and Princes by name as they walked out onto the stage. He felt his cheeks warm as Vanessa walked out wearing a deep purple sarong dress, her dimples framed by two strands of hair that flowed by her face, the rest tied in a bun.

After they were all introduced, The Band started up and The Cheerleaders made their way to the stage while The Princesses took the hands of their designated Princes. Everyone began to dance.

The Citizens cheered and clapped as The Cheerleaders performed their routine, throwing members into the air, creating stunning spectacles.

The Royals walked into the crowd, encouraging The Children to join in with the dances, inviting parents, too. Vanessa locked eyes with Blaine and her Prince spun her away towards him.

He shook his head as she took his hands and dragged him past the cheering public. He danced as she tried to lead him.

They both heard Brooke's belly laugh from across the crowd as she skipped over and joined.

The three doubled up in laughter at each other's improvised dance moves.

As the routines came to an end, the crowds applauded the skill of The Cheerleaders and the clowning of The Royalty. Brooke and Vanessa dragged Blaine up on stage. The Mayor handed the microphone over to Brooke to make the next announcement.

She pulled Blaine over with her.

"Ladies and Gents, this wonderful and beautiful man by my side is one of my colleagues at Kestrel. If you want to see some more of his dance moves, I am sure he will be showing them off tonight while he pours your drinks."

A cheer arose from the crowd.

"This is his first year at Our Festival, as I'm sure it is for some of you. He's been in this community for a short time and is already a big part of Our Family here."

Amanda chanted his name in a deep voice from under the gazebo.

"So let's make this special for all of those, like him, who have worked hard this year!"

Blaine waved as Vanessa took his hand and pulled him to her side.

The festivities continued and Amanda took her break, allowing Blaine a chance to catch up on their competition.

The events and games, hosted by The Princesses and The Princes, finished up as the crowd shrank. People made their way to the parks for barbecues, or home to refuel and get ready for the evening's events.

~~~

The intense evening sun was now burning bright, producing a palette of colour across the sky. Kestrel's doors re-opened and a gentle flow of people entered the bar.

They set the upstairs bar as VIP for The Royals and those who took part in the parade, of legal drinking age, of course.

The top bar was quiet for the first half hour so Blaine, still behind on the bet, snuck down to the main bar to try and rein in some more tips. By 10:00 the queue outside stretched around the corner; there was still no sign of the girls. Blaine cleared glasses, heading upstairs to check how things were going. Mel was making cocktail after cocktail so Amanda did the bar swap.

The beautiful evening sky rolled over into a dark night sky, becoming the perfect backdrop for those standing out on the balcony across from the bar. Everyone was relaxed and respectful, patient and polite. Even The Mayor, who was definitely past the point of tipsy, was mingling, dancing, and causing mischief.

Blaine continued pouring drinks as the evening went on into night and the girls showed up with an awkward Vanessa and Demi between a tense Brooke and Katie.

"Good evening, ladies," he said, Vanessa leaning over the bar to kiss him. "What can I get for you?"

"Three shots of tequila," Brooke chimed in.

Vanessa added, "And two ciders."

"Margarita." Katie stood, her arms crossed.

Blaine cracked open the two ciders and poured one of the shots, which Brooke took before the liquid settled. She slammed it down, so he poured the next two into the same glass, and then began to make the margarita as Demi and Brooke walked out onto the balcony.

Katie leaned on the bar, finger tapping, looking over at Brooke. Blaine mouthed to Vanessa, cider in hand, "What happened?"

She mouthed back, her body stiff, "Later."

He watched as Demi and Brooke made their way to the

stairs. Katie swiped her drink and walked over to a group across the room, leaving Vanessa to catch up with the other two before they disappeared.

"I'm on a roll today!" said Amanda, sneaking up behind Blaine and making him jump.

He looked out over the top bar; the girls were all out of view.

"Don't feel too confident."

"Nahhhhhh, I'm literally on fire! Trust boy, you ain't catching me. But I'll give you a chance, otherwise it's no fun. Swapsies?"

Blaine went down to help out Mel, Tim, and the part-timers, all the while keeping his eyes out for the girls.

The dancefloor was full, people showcasing their best and worst moves. Brooke and Demi were getting on like friends reunited after years apart, Vanessa mingling with the girls and guys from the parade.

The main bar was much busier than the top bar, the staff ducking and diving past each other for drinks and card machines, so Blaine went out onto the floor to do a glass run.

He ended up managing to dance with the girls to Lynyrd Skynyrd — Free Bird, the three of them upbeat without Katie. Blaine's moves attracted the attention of The Mayor, who stumbled over to dance with him. Tim laughed behind the bar, bringing attention towards this scene.

As the night continued, Blaine spotted Brooke and Danny in a heated conversation on the balcony. Then, noticing Katie come upstairs and head over to the two, he felt a dark cloud form.

Continuing to serve, he kept the corner of his eye on them, witnessing Brooke throw her hands up in the air and make her way over to the bar. Her emotions trembled through her face.

She slinked around the back of the bar to be out of view.

Mel had noticed the three as well, and gave a nod to Blaine.

"Hey BeeBee, you all good?" he asked.

She attempted to give Blaine one of her smiles but her tearful eyes betrayed her.

"I'm fine, I just needed to go somewhere quiet for a sec." She looked at him for a moment and her lip began to quiver.

Blaine held out his arms and she leaped forward, bursting into tears, burying herself into his chest.

"It shouldn't bother me," she sobbed. "Why does it bother me?"

"Because you're human and you're allowed to be sad."

"But I don't care!"

"I know," he said, stroking her hair.

"Bartenders really do make great therapists," she chuckled through her tears. "But friends are even better."

He wiped her cheek. "Let's get you some water, hey?"

"Double vodka on ice? Pleassse?"

"Of course, Ma'am."

Red eyed, Brooke choked a laugh.

As Blaine escorted her to the front of the bar and made her drink, Danny saw them. He cut through the queue.

"Oi! Word of advice, dude. Don't get caught between those two girls. They'll both play you for The Jerk."

Blaine didn't acknowledge him.

"Don't ignore me!" Danny slammed his hands on the counter, drawing the attention of everyone in the bar, who pretended to continue their conversations while watching like vultures.

Blaine looked up at him. "I think you need to just take a step back, okay buddy."

"Buddy!"

Brooke curled her chin down to her chest.

"Danny, step outside and take a breath. Then come back in here and talk to me and The Festival's Queen with a little respect, okay?"

Danny's jaw clenched. "Fuck you!"

Now seeing Brooke becoming more uncomfortable, Blaine walked along the bar, luring Danny away.

"Who do you think you are?" Danny spouted. "Why don't you take a step back and stop intervening in things that don't concern you, okay, buddy?"

"You make it my concern when you approach my bar the way you did." Blaine's voice grew edges. "But you make it my priority when you upset my friend the way you have. I really think the best thing for you to do right now is to step outside."

By this point, Tim was at the top of the stairs on standby while Mel came back behind the bar and Amanda walked around the balcony, collecting glasses.

"You see what you do!" a drunk Katie gestured to Brooke. "You have all the boys fighting over you and you pretend to be innocent all of a sudden."

Brooke was backed against the bar, shaken.

Tim put his hand on her shoulder. Katie scoffed and walked over to Danny, who was still yelling at Blaine. She took Danny's hand and whispered in his ear.

He glared at Blaine before saying, "Neither of them are fucking worth it, mate. Trust me. I can speak from experience." His glare turned to Brooke.

Blaine clenched his fist up on the counter. He reached to grab Danny, but before he could, Amanda, behind Danny and Katie, placed her hands on their backs, and ordered, "Out." She marched them towards the stairs.

Tim comforted Brooke and apologised to the guests who were watching the events unfold. He walked around the back of the bar to Blaine. "Do a glass run, walk it off. I'll take over here for a bit, B." Blaine took a deep breath and nodded. "Also, take Brooke back to her friends." Tim turned to her. "Her true friends."

The great thing about big events is that so much happens, people quickly forget and move onto the next thing, which, in this case, was The Mayor's trousers splitting on the dancefloor.

By 2:45, people made their way out into the night, arms linked with new friends, lips locked with new lovers.

Tim walked over to Blaine and Amanda.

"You two call it a night. I'll thank you both properly in the morning. Enjoy the rest of your night," he said, shaking their hands. "And … Just come in whenever tomorrow." Tim patted them both on the back.

"Final count?" Blaine asked.

"Eighty-three …" Amanda paused to count the change, "Fifty."

"Eighty-three fifty! Nice, I'm on around sixty-four."

"Sucker! But good effort, all things considering." Amanda tipped her head to the side.

As they grabbed their stuff from around the back, Tim told them to pick up a case of beers on their way out.

Blaine found the girls outside. They all agreed to wait while Amanda collected the case before heading for The Hill.

It seemed like the perfect way to end the evening.

The Princess

Now, a lot happened on the day of The Festival. So let's see the day again from another perspective.

Saturday morning gently woke The Princess. Rolling over to hug the body beside her and feeling nobody there, she remembered she'd spent the night in her own bed.

She rubbed her eyes and mentally prepared for the day ahead. Her body clock had woken her early. She figured she could get in a quick jog before she started work, so decided to take a different route this morning, taking her work clothes in a rucksack.

The Princess set off in the opposite direction to usual and meandered through the neighbouring streets a few blocks over. As she passed a couple of bungalows, she noticed a girl, heels in hand, sneaking around the side of one of them.

Katie? She dismissed the thought and disappeared around the corner.

Vanessa got to The Cafe, where Jenny and Mick were already set to open. Dean and his boyfriend arrived a couple minutes after and they all stood by the counter, taking deep breaths as the first family came in.

And just like that, it all began.

Family after family, couple after couple, people parked up on the street across, all starting their day here before heading to town to get the best spot.

Vanessa and Jenny were so busy, neither noticed Blaine arrive, but Vanessa felt a little of her worry and stress disappear upon seeing his face.

She couldn't help her eyes from wandering over to Blaine in his baggy hoodie as he chatted with guests and served them, wearing the truest smile across his face. The stress from the morning rush took her mind away from the nerves for the day. But with the rush now ending, they returned. Vanessa caught her reflection in the window and felt the sweat on her forehead, realising she couldn't go to The Festival like this.

Vanessa walked up to the apartment, leaving her clothes on the arm of the sofa, and hopped in the shower to refresh.

She heard Blaine outside, getting changed into his work clothes for the day. He called through the door. "Lock up when you're done, Vans. Enjoy today, love you." And then she heard the front door close.

Love you too. She turned the shower off.

Vanessa stepped out and dried herself, letting her hair down to brush it out. When she came out of the bathroom she saw that Blaine had folded her work clothes for her and left a note on top:

I'm already proud of you for finding
your courage again and today is proof
of that
I know you are nervous but you don't
need to be
Just relax and enjoy the day

She put the note in her bag, left Blaine's apartment, and locked the door.

Brooke met Vanessa outside the high school and the two

walked in to meet the rest of The Royals. As they went through the reception and signed in, Brooke turned to Vanessa and remarked, "Life's funny, huh."

Vanessa returned a raised eyebrow.

"This time last year I stood here with Katie and had completely forgotten you even existed. This time eight years ago I stood here with you while you signed in for the band and I signed in for the cheerleaders, convincing you to join them for the following year. I just think that's funny, don't you? Life has this way of, I guess, repeating itself. But with differences you could never have predicted. You never really know how things will turn out. They just kind of ... do."

"This day last year I worked like every other day and then went home. I can't even remember what I did. I remember my parents heading out in the evening and I think I just cooked tacos or something," Vanessa said. "If you'd have told me in a year's time I'd be standing next to Brooke Bennett, as friends again, I'd probably have choked on that taco."

The faint sound of voices could be heard as Vanessa signed her name.

"These past few months have been really eye opening," she said, putting the pen down. "I'd lost any sense of direction for my life and had given up. But I've realised that yeah, life just kind of happens without you even trying. Even in the times I thought nothing important was happening. The little things all add up now and guide you. I just needed to embrace them and get out of my comfort zone."

"The little things add up and guide you," Brooke pondered. "That's so true. I've been looking back on the past few years and beating myself up over the person I was, but you're right. There were always little things that I ignored for too long."

"Have to listen to your gut."

They arrived in the girls' locker room and got ready with the rest of The Queens, Princesses, and Cheerleaders. Meeting the rest of the festival party outside in the courtyard, they went through the schedule for the day before walking into town.

The parade began.

Vanessa danced with Blaine in the crowd, her first experience as The Princess. After the crowd dispersed, she and Brooke made their way to the game they were hosting — The Sack Race.

She followed Brooke's lead when it came to interacting with the people. Brooke was light, fun, and gentle as she got the kids to participate. Vanessa had convinced a group of young girls, as well as a group of men in their early thirties, to join in.

Now with the teams set, the race could start.

The men took some big leaps into the lead, but resorted to sabotaging each other, much to the amusement of the crowd. As the men all ended up on the ground in hysterics, one of the little boys took the lead and won the first round.

After the first few games finished, it was time for the next section of the parade, The Royals' dance routines. That went without a hitch and the crowd applauded as The Royals bowed and announced the next section of the day.

Vanessa took a moment to catch her thoughts, alone. Then she spotted Katie across the street and was about to head over when she noticed who she was with. Katie pecked Danny on the lips before taking a sip from his beer. Vanessa walked on, away from them.

Fuck sake, she thought, realising she had to tell Brooke. *A few months ago I'd have laughed at the irony and karma of this, but Brooke's my friend now ... she should know, right?*

Vanessa spent the rest of the afternoon avoiding both

Brooke and Katie. She didn't want to stir anything. Karma would work its magic.

As the events for the day came to an end, the girls headed back to Brooke's to get ready for the evening. Vanessa had invited Demi who showed up with pizza and a bottle of wine.

She introduced Demi to Katie and Brooke.

The music started and so did the dancing — John Mayer, New Light.

Demi helped Brooke with her hair as she did her make-up, and Vanessa dove straight into the pizza box and Katie straight into the cider case.

"So who do you plan to go home with tonight, Katie?" asked Brooke.

"We'll see what the talent is like first."

"So not that guy I saw you with in town earlier?" Demi asked. "Is he just a bit of fun?"

Brooke's jaw dropped. "You didn't tell me you had someone already on the go!"

Katie sniggered. "You've been distant since I came back so it never really came up. It's just a bit of fun while I'm back for the summer, anyway."

"How has it not come up?" Brooke chided. "That's all you talk about. So who is he?"

"He's no one, just a bit of fun."

Brooke and Demi looked at each other in the mirror and smiled.

"Okay, Okay," Brooke said, taking a sip from her drink.

Demi whispered in Brooke's ear, "Well, if he is going tonight, I'm sure we'll find out anyway."

Vanessa said nothing and ate her pizza. Karma would work its magic.

The Girls finished getting ready, Vanessa now in her peach dress, and they called a taxi.

Katie received a text from one of The Princesses.

> 9:53: Where u girls @? Its so crowded and couldn't find you in the queue.

She went outside to call them.

When they pulled up, the queue was wrapping around the corner. Luckily, since they were on the VIP list, they only had to wait a couple minutes to get in.

As they walked through the door, Demi spotted Danny. Vanessa saw Demi's eyes light up. She felt her stomach churn. *This can't happen to Brooke ... not tonight.*

Vanessa knew she had to intervene. But before she could stop her, Demi elbowed Brooke.

"That's the guy."

"What?"

"That guy there, that's Katie's bit of fun." Demi chuckled, expecting Brooke to join her.

She did not.

"That's my ex ..."

Demi's face dropped. Brooke marched over to Katie, who was saying hello to the other Princesses.

"Danny?" Brooke asked, her eyes burning as her voice pushed through clenched teeth.

Katie looked at her, confused, "What about him?"

"He is your 'bit of fun'?" Brooke tried to remain calm.

Katie looked over to the two girls as Demi gave an uncomfortable smile.

"Shit," Katie said under her breath.

Brooke's voice was modulated, her face masked in false humour.

"Oh, you've got to be fucking kidding me!" She turned and grabbed Demi's arm. "I need a drink!"

Vanessa looked over at Katie and the two followed them up, and well, you know what happens next.

The evening flew by for Vanessa, despite the drama that surrounded her. She danced and laughed with her friends. Demi introduced her to The Photographer she had mentioned. He talked her through the job he wanted to hire her for. It sounded perfect. It was the next step she needed.

Before Vanessa knew it, they were all leaving. She and Blaine went with Amanda in her car; Demi, Brooke, and a couple of The Princesses and Princes took a taxi.

Some of The Cheerleaders and The Sports Team were already on The Hill having their own party as the two cars arrived.

Blaine cracked open a beer and watched Vanessa in the company of her new friends. She smiled over at him, finishing up her conversation before she came to sit beside him.

The two looked out over Wayton's streetlights.

"Hello, stranger. How are you feeling?" he asked, as she took his hand.

"I'm so tired!" she groaned. "But I'm having the best night. How's your day been?"

"Nice. Really nice."

She saw his eyes watching out over The Hill, towards the sky.

"Good!"

"I like it here," Blaine said, turning his gaze to the stars.

"It's a good spot. I haven't been here since high school, though. Too many memories I wanted to forget. But I guess tonight will redeem that."

They sat, not speaking, just listening to the voices and sounds that surrounded them.

Vanessa broke into a soft giggle.

Blaine turned to her. "What?"

"This night's a perfect shade of Dark Blue."

He grinned and then looked up at the stars glittering across the royal blue night sky.

Blaine sang softly, "Have you ever been alone in a crowded room, when I'm here with you? I said the world could be burning, burning down."

Vanessa joined in and they sang the chorus together.

Vanessa hummed a while longer, resting her head on Blaine's shoulder. "Six months ago ... If you had told me that the raggedy stranger with the sexy accent would ask me out on a date, I'd become his hair stylist, fall in love with him, become friends with Brooke Bennett, be one of this year's Festival Princesses and have, not just a plan for my life, but a way to actually pursue it ... I'd have laughed you out of The Cafe."

Blaine's face lit up. "What did Demi's friend say?"

"He is The Photographer for a travel magazine and has been hired to make an advertisement article for a group of hotels. He wants to hire me for a fashion shoot out in Bali! It's like a two-week thing, expenses paid, and it pays really well!"

Blaine's smile was luminous. "That's so good!"

"I'm not sure though." Her face fell into a frown.

He squeezed her hand. "Why not? It sounds perfect."

"Two weeks on my own, with strangers. I'm not sure how I'd cope."

"You're kidding ... you'll be fine. I think you'd be crazy not to jump at this opportunity. Sometimes you just need to take that leap of faith in life and see where it takes you. Trust me."

Blaine got to his feet and Vanessa held onto his hand, pulling herself up, too.

"It is daunting, I know, but the result is always worth it. Six months ago you'd never have imagined any of this." Blaine gestured to the crowd of strangers she'd just spent her day laughing with. "Hell, neither would I. I was expecting to last like a month, but life has a funny way of working out perfectly."

Vanessa cast an eye over to Brooke, who was lying with Demi.

Blaine continued, "It holds out these moments every now and then. And if you don't take them, you end up static, which is fine if you're in a place you want to be. But I see it in your eyes. You are on a climb in life that is filling you with so much happiness and you are nowhere near its peak, so please don't stop this journey because you're anxious about what might happen. Embrace the unpredictability of what could happen."

"That seems to be the theme of today." Vanessa swung his arms.

As she stood facing him, she felt the cool summer breeze caress her neck. Vanessa looked into Blaine's eyes. They were alight: brightly shining and weightless as a feather.

And in that moment she saw the reason he always seemed naturally calm and collected ... he wasn't.

He was exactly like she was. It was Yalena who had given him this view. Blaine was still filled with anxieties just as Vanessa was, but rather than being scared by the "what if?" he was empowered by the "what might?"

"Okay," she said, as her eyes gained a twinkle. "I'm going to Bali to model for a magazine ..." Her dimples spread across her face.

"You'll say yes?"

"Yeah ..." She froze, staring into space, and then her eyes looked back at him. "It doesn't seem real ..."

"Reality often doesn't."

She giggled, and he pulled her in close, spinning her around to rest his chin on her head, as they looked out to the horizon.

The Queen

Now, a lot happened on the day of The Festival. So let's see the day again from one more perspective.

On the morning of The Festival, The Girl awoke as The Queen, for the first and only day.

She opened her eyes and felt the power of the day energize her body. Passing her mother, she placed a kiss on her cheek.

"Excited for the day, Brooke?"

"Yeah, it's going to be fun," she replied, skipping downstairs for breakfast.

"Me and your father are going to a party after the festivities so you and the girls can come back here to get ready for the night," her mother called down.

"Awesome! Thanks."

Brooke made herself a bowl of oats and fruit and sat out on the doorstep, bathing in the energy as she watched groups of people pass.

She went down to the shops to grab some drinks and snacks for later, then, drawing the beauty mark on her cheek, walked to the school to meet Vanessa.

When the girls arrived in town, Brooke was getting ready to do her first announcement when she heard voices calling, "Jenifer!" from the crowd.

She knew it was for her.

Brooke turned around to see Tommy, Abby, and the group walking over.

"Jenifer! It's so crowded it's crazy. How have we never heard of this before? We didn't think we'd find you." Tommy walked over and gave her a hug.

"I can't believe you guys actually came!"

Katie and Vanessa looked at each other, stunned.

"So how have you guys been?" Brooke asked.

"Good! Excited for today," said Abby.

"Well, I've got to go do an announcement, but come find me at one of the games later on! I'll get you involved." Brooke winked.

Tommy agreed, taking Abby by the hand, and disappeared off into the crowd.

Katie asked, "So what was that about?"

Brooke smirked. "I went on a weekend trip last month and met them. Told them to come. I didn't think they would, though."

Vanessa's mouth hung open as she processed what just happened. "I can't believe you are still Jenifering people."

"I do it all the time!" Katie added, "Honestly still the best way to get away with mischief."

"I forget how much we used to do that at the Wayton house parties!" Vanessa said.

"Man, those were days!" Katie threw her arms around the two girls' waists. "We were actually a pretty awesome trio ... I forget that."

Vanessa tried not to think about it. "That's another lifetime ago for me!"

Hopefully it will be for me too, soon, Brooke thought.

Up on stage, Brooke made her first announcement and watched as Blaine and Vanessa danced together, eyes locked. She felt a warmth in her face, seeing Vanessa happy and content.

After she and Vanessa hosted the sack race, she left Vanessa, with confidence, to go and host her next game alone. Brooke went to find Katie for their next duty as Queens — to judge the fashion competition.

They watched as middle-aged women strutted across the stage, their husbands, wives, and friends cheering them on in their moment in the spotlight. Katie and Brooke sat on their thrones, laughing and cheering as well, Katie's sly comments not adding to the humour. After they crowned the fashion icon, Katie turned to Brooke.

"I've missed hanging out with you lately, girl! Sucks you're so busy."

Returning a smile, Brooke thought to herself, *I really don't miss this as much as I used to … I like how things have been lately.*

Walking through the crowds, and occasionally asked to be part of a photo, Brooke watched the groups of young teens hanging out, laughing, and playing around.

It used to be that easy. But, I mean, it still is if I do it right.

At one point she saw Tilly with a group of guys around her. It was like looking back in time. Brooke wished she could un-teach some of the lessons she had imparted to Tilly. She realised, though, that these were lessons she, herself, had to unlearn, so she knew Tilly would, too. Quickly, Brooke hoped.

As the events for the day came to an end, the girls headed back to Brooke's to get ready for the evening. Demi showed up with pizza and wine, the music started, and the events began.

After Vanessa introduced her to Katie and Brooke, Demi told Brooke the stories she had heard from Vanessa, and Brooke apologised.

"Hey, we all need to grow," Demi said. "I used to be such a bitch when I first entered the industry, but you get to a point where it's not fun making people feel like shit. You realise how amazing it feels to boost your girls up instead."

"Yeah ... think I've started to figure that out."

"Everyone loves a redemption arc! Shows that anyone can be worthy of positive change. They just have to make the effort!"

The girls were nearly ready so Brooke finished her bottle of vodka with some help from Vanessa and Demi, while Katie went outside to call The Princesses that were already at Kestrel.

"So my friend that works for the fashion line loved you two today," Demi said, wincing from the vodka. "They've been looking for someone fresh to be the face of their new campaign."

Brooke turned to Vanessa. "That's so great, V!"

"Actually Brooke, they loved you. They loved your charisma and confidence and how you let your personality show on stage. And the way you interacted with people is exactly what they need. They want to talk with you tomorrow before they leave."

Vanessa's brows lifted. "Brooke, that's awesome! You can finally get yourself out of this town like you want to!"

"But I feel bad ... this was your moment!"

Demi cut in. "Don't feel bad! The Photographer I invited is planning a shoot in Bali and he wants to speak with Vans tonight about getting involved."

"You're playing! Bali?" Vanessa's eyes beamed.

The two girls sat on Brooke's sofa, stunned into silence.

"Yo ... Fuck ..." Which were about the only two words Brooke could manage.

She gulped down the last of her drink. "Okay, I can't process this right now ... When do they want to meet?"

"I said I'd ask you. They leave early evening tomorrow, though." Demi was warmed by the bewildered look on Brooke's face. "I'll let them know. Where?"

"The Cafe?" Vanessa suggested. "That way I can support you as well."

"Agreed?" Demi asked.

Brooke nodded. "Agreed."

Katie poked her head around the door to tell them the taxi for Kestrel had arrived.

"Tonight is amazing! I'm not going to forget this. Thank you, V," Brooke whispered.

When they pulled up, the queue wrapped around the corner. Brooke couldn't stop smiling. She was expecting the usual mischievous antics, followed by a lot of drinking and mild regret in the morning. Instead, the morning wasn't going to hold regret, but a step forward. Not even a step, a stride.

They walked through the door and found the group of Festival Royals on the edge of the dancefloor.

Brooke felt Demi nudge her.

"That's the guy."

Brooke turned to her, confused. "What?"

"That guy there is Katie's bit of fun."

She felt her skin go cold. "That's my ex …"

Demi's face dropped. Brooke marched over to Katie.

"Danny?"

Katie looked at her, confused. "What about him?"

"He is your 'bit of fun'?"

"Shit."

"Oh, you've got to be fucking kidding me!" Brooke turned and grabbed Demi's arm. "I need a drink!"

She dragged Demi upstairs. Brooke plowed her way to the front of the bar. Demi and Vanessa created a barrier between her and Katie. Just in case.

"Look, Brooke, let me explain." That was Katie.

"Oh, fuck off," Brooke said, resisting the vodkas.

"It just sort of happened one night," Katie argued. Brooke stayed quiet.

Then there was Blaine. "Good evening, ladies. What can I get for you?"

"Three shots of tequila …"

"And two ciders."

"Margarita."

Brooke took the shots, feeling each burn in her throat, then walked out to the balcony. Demi followed.

"I actually can't believe her!" Brooke said. "But I can! It's Katie. Of course she'd jump on him as soon as I was out the picture! I don't want to be with him anymore, but you know, there are rules to avoid this sort of shit! Feelings don't just disappear."

"It's never easy. The last girl I was with was only a few months but even that still lingers. How long were you with him?"

"Nearly five years …"

"Fuck that bitch!" Demi exclaimed. "So she's been friends with you the entire time you were with him?"

"Yeah! … I guess it's karma though … for what I did to Vanessa."

"No, come on. Even Vanessa told me it was more rumour than anything. Not to mention high school drama is allowed to be dumb and over dramatic. But this bitch is supposed to be an adult."

Brooke's thoughts trembled through her body.

"Let's go dance." Demi took Brooke's hand. "Take your mind off this for a bit." They walked back in and towards the stairs as Vanessa caught up.

The girls danced. Brooke enjoyed the attention from Demi between trips to the bar.

Danny and Brooke ended up shoulder to shoulder at the bar, unaware of each other, until he heard her voice.

"It feels like you've been avoiding me lately."

Brooke felt her stomach twist. "Yeah. I have. How's Katie?"

"She's with you, isn't she?"

"Is she? I thought she was in your bed?" Brooke grabbed her drink and made her way through the crowd.

Danny pushed after her. "Brooke, just listen. Let me explain."

She stopped.

Taking a breath, Brooke led him up to the balcony so they could talk. Leaning on the wall, she focused her gaze — out — over the town. She knew looking at him would break her calm.

His words were gentle. "I know I'm a jerk, but it happened so fast. We were drunk and I was hurting and confused and she comforted me … She made me feel like it was going to be okay. I spent every week back at Uni thinking about you, trying to convince myself it wasn't over. Then I came back and it was clear you'd moved on … and Katie made me feel good again."

Brooke was silent.

"I miss … I love you."

Brooke's eyes turned to the street below. "I'm not mad at you … I'm angry at Katie. I ended things so you have every right to move on. But don't tell me you love me after you've spent the past few weeks fucking my best friend."

"Come on, Brooke. You've been avoiding both of us! You say you're best friends but where have you been? Here with that dick behind the bar and Gretchen."

"This has nothing to do with them! I've been avoiding you because it became obvious just how toxic you both are! … Fuck sake." She shook her head and laughed at the ground, finding a calm in her voice. "Why couldn't I have realised it all those years ago, just like Vanessa did?"

Katie came up the stairs. "Oh, you two are so gonna hook up tonight, then? So much drama!" Katie slurred.

Brooke scoffed at her, but Danny responded to Brooke.

"Toxic? How are we the toxic ones! You are the one always playing games and now all of a sudden you stop and we are supposed to just believe that. You're manipulative, Brooke! How was I supposed to have trusted you?"

"Oh! You're blaming me for trust? You tried to hook up with my best friend a year into our relationship and I took your side. And now, here you are, years later, hooking up with another one of my best friends. And this is all somehow my fault?"

"Hardly your best friend though, am I?" Katie said, standing close to Danny. "You're too busy trying to be part of a relationship you'll never have."

"Everything was fine until that outsider showed up," Danny spat.

"Everything was not fine!" Brooke spat back. "We normalised a fucked-up situation because we didn't know any better. This has nothing to do with Blaine or Vanessa at all! The only thing they've made me aware of is that I can be better. But you guys haven't figured that out yet because you are so caught up with your fucking egos!"

Katie spoke. "You're never gonna fuck The Bartender, Brooke. Just accept it."

"You aren't even listening to what I'm saying," Brooke laughed. "I've just figured out how I can actually and genuinely be happy and not pretend anymore."

Danny screwed up his face. "So what did you figure out? Causing drama makes you happy? Is that what comes next? You cause drama between those two and when everyone is unhappy, then Brooke is happy?"

Brooke felt her body tighten. "How did I cause this drama? I've had nothing to do with either of you for months!"

Katie and Danny kept talking at Brooke, neither of them listening.

Brooke sighed. She put her hands up in surrender.

"Fuck this," her lip began to quiver. "I don't need this anymore … I'd finally gotten past it and here I am being sucked back into this petty, immature bullshit!" and she walked away from the two most important people of her past, towards the most important person in her present.

"You think you're so much better than us don't you, bitch!" Katie spat out.

Demi was proving to be the perfect new ally tonight. The two girls fell into the back of the six-person taxi. One of The Princes laughed and announced out into the street of faces, "Ladies and Gentlemen! Your Queen!"

The people clapped as Brooke found her way to her feet and took a bow. That grin broke into her signature smile as she addressed her citizens.

"The Queen wishes you all a goodnight! Return home safe, my loyal subjects!"

They all laughed as the doors slid shut on the applause.

Brooke guided The Driver out of the town, towards The Hill, reassuring him as they directed him down the country road.

Pulling up just after Vanessa, Amanda, and Blaine, they all helped themselves to a beer from the case Tim had gifted. Brooke and the girls continued to dance to the music being played from somebody's crackling phone speaker, breaking off for drunken heart-to-hearts until a good song came back on.

Demi lay down to look up at the stars as she spoke. "You're a good soul, you know that?"

"I haven't been." Brooke was beginning to sober up. "But I'm really trying to change that."

She lay down beside Demi.

"Just because you've done bad things doesn't mean you aren't a good soul. Just means you've been struggling to find your way." Demi turned her head to look at Brooke. "You have a good soul, Brooke Bennett … Embrace it more, it looks good on you."

Blaine and Vanessa cosied up, Blaine's head touching Brooke's, Vanessa's against Demi's. Demi welcomed them to the conversation.

"Vans?"

Vanessa, still tipsy, hummed as a response.

"Tell Brooke she has a good soul."

Vanessa took a breath, preparing for her speech.

"Brooke Bethany Bennett, even though you've been a bitch to me in the past, your smile is irrefutably beautiful and spreads joy wherever it is cast. If that isn't the sign of a good soul, I don't know what is."

Blaine agreed. "When I first met you, everyone warned me you were trouble. But I saw me in that smile, the one who was lost. But someone, who will always be in my heart, helped guide me to a better place. They saw how much I wanted to break the cycle. I saw your soul shine through, just the same. You've just gotta let it free."

He sat up and raised his bottle.

"Find the things that matter. The traditions, the memories, the people, the small things, and hold them tight. Moments like this are why we are here. Enjoy them."

The four watched the stars dance above them.

Vanessa broke the silence. "BeeBee?"

She hadn't heard Vanessa call her that in years. Brooke responded with a gentle hum.

"Do you remember the old tradition?" Vanessa asked.

"Of course."

Blaine chuckled. "Okay, good, so it is a thing. Brooke didn't just make it up."

Vanessa sat up. "Wait, how do you know it?"

"My first month here, she brought me up and made me do it."

Vanessa's eyes burned into him. "Oh … I see!"

Brooke's giggle broke into her belly laugh, sparking Blaine and Vanessa into laughter.

Demi asked, "What old tradition?"

Brooke got to her feet, pulled the straps down off her shoulders, lowered the top half of her dress, and shouted.

"Fuck Wayton!"

Vanessa joined in, flashing, followed by Blaine who pulled his trousers down.

Demi shrugged, jumped to her feet, and joined them.

A cheer erupted from everyone on The Hill. Soon they were all exposing different parts of themselves to the streetlights of the sleeping town.

And thus, it was passed on.

As the sun began to rise, Blaine glanced over to Brooke who returned the look. They all sat and watched before clearing up the litter and mess they had made so they could leave The Hill as they had found it.

Untouched and beautiful.

~~~

Next morning day broke through the blinds. Rolling out of bed and stumbling to the bathroom to pee, she looked in the mirror. The night before had been long and stressful. A rough, tired face grimaced back, barely visible through half-open eyes. She splashed some water to wake that face up.

Same old shit, she smiled at the face in the mirror. *But it's over now.*

Closing her eyes, she stumbled back to the room, picking up clothes scattered over the floor, got changed, and headed downstairs. The Queen grabbed a brownie and a smoothie and looked at the time — 8:32.

She groaned.

"It's too early, man!" But taking a deep breath, she made her way to work, powered by a generous three hours' sleep.

She walked through the door early, the first one to show. Tim popped his head around the corner, his laugh rumbling through Brooke's head.

"The Queen in all her morning glory. Even after a big night out you don't fail to look gorgeous, Brooke."

She squinted back, unimpressed, knowing the truth of how she really looked.

"People need to stop being so kind to me lately. It'll go to my head."

"It can join all those double vodkas that I'm sure are making your head pulse right now."

She stuck out her tongue, and got straight to work cleaning, reorganising, and stocking up the bar with the other staff unlucky enough to have pulled the short straw.

She arrived home, Tim having decided to show mercy. Brooke set an alarm, passed straight out, waking up to make herself some lunch before meeting Demi at The Cafe for her interview.

Her new Title pending.

The Citizens

The last few weeks of summer were calm, with only a few rainy days. The Festival was still fresh in everyone's minds and attitudes. The Citizens walked the streets with relaxed purpose, be it a new-found path or relieved soul, renewed from the events. All were content again.

Outed as The Jerk and The Bitch, The Knight and The Courtesan shared a few weeks of passion before going their separate ways, neither able to shake their new reality.

The Princess only wore her title for those following weeks, but it wasn't long before she settled back into her role as The Servant Girl. She had missed the quiet contentment that came with being The Nerd in her private life and The Model away from public eyes. Royalty brought too much attention for her.

At the end of a regular day, Vanessa left work and spent the evening with Brooke and Blaine. She sat on the sofa beside Blaine, Brooke in the kitchen making popcorn. This was her life now, and she knew, whatever the future held, it would be great.

The Girl was finding her feet. First in steps, then in strides. She felt weightless yet grounded. Brooke overcame each anxiety, thanks to the people around her reminding her, "You got this. You are The Queen." She quit her job at the home-ware store. It was a chapter she was happy to close; she had the Kestrel family now.

The Outsider was no more. It seemed everyone had forgotten a time when Blaine was a stranger. He was The Bartender at Kestrel, that friendly, smiling face that poured your drinks and listened to your troubles.

He looked back over the better half of a year and felt a warmth in his chest. *To think I had stumbled across this place a few years ago with Yalena,* he thought, while polishing glasses on a quiet shift at the end of the summer.

What was supposed to be a refuel and lunch had turned into a wander. He and Yalena had talked about eventually settling down in a place like this, a little house with a couple of kids.

Yalena had teased him. "But we are bus people now. We will never have a life like that. How are we supposed to settle down when we know there is a whole world out there waiting to be seen?"

"We have years before we even have to start thinking of settling down," he replied.

"Kids would be nice, though," Yalena had said as they walked past The Basketball Court. "Teach them to admire the hidden beauty in the world."

He blinked away a tear as he checked the shine on the next glass, Brooke noticing.

"Are you okay, B?"

"Yeah."

"Whatcha thinkin'?"

"Just reflecting. This time last year I wasn't in a good place and didn't think it would ever get better. Now here I am … Happy." His voice cracked.

Brooke had forgotten about Blaine's unspoken past.

"Sorry, I don't know why it's getting to me today." Blaine chuckled.

"It's okay, Blaine. As long as they are happy tears."

"They are. They really are. I've been floating through life these past years and this is the first time I've really stopped to think. I'm grateful to have found gravity again." He turned to Brooke with the biggest smile he could muster. "I've become a citizen."

Brooke returned that smile only she could give. "I'm hoping I'll find this gravity you speak of. I think I am beginning to."

Blaine looked around at the few people in the bar, most there to keep out of the gentle rainfall. Reaching up to the top shelf, he took down the bottle of cherry vodka and poured two shots.

"Here's to the autumn. May it bring health and happiness that lead into the winter and all the days that follow."

They clinked their glasses together.

~~~

The summer days drew to a close and autumn took the spotlight. The Citizens' routines returned to normal as the trees turned to gold. Brooke spent most of the weekdays at her brother's, coming back at the weekend for work.

Vanessa met Brooke in the city after a photo-shoot and interview to make arrangements for Bali. Brooke had suggested she stay the night rather than catch the bus back.

The two went for dinner at a burger restaurant, Buns of Beauty, and ordered two chili burgers with fries to share. Vanessa had a cream soda and Brooke started off with water but ordered a cherry soda when the food arrived.

"So how's it going with the fashion line stuff?" Vanessa

asked as she took a handful of fries, eating them one by one from her palm.

"Yeah, really well. I've modelled a couple of pieces that are stunning! They had me do an interview for an 'about me' section in the company magazine, which was weird."

"What sort of things did you talk about?"

"I don't even know." Brooke grimaced. "I just blabbed about a load of shit probably. I mentioned the fact this was a fresh start for me after a year of working and living for a paycheck, and they wanted me to talk about that a bit more. So I said how I've spent the year working on myself and how I was grateful it was starting to take a positive effect."

Brooke bit into the burger as Vanessa began to speak.

"That's good. It's relatable! I think so many people spend a lot of time just floating, unsure on the next move they need to make. Maybe you'll inspire some readers to do the same thing you've done."

Swallowing, wiping the corners of her mouth with her thumb and finger, Brooke put the burger down.

"It's nice to have been given a platform to have a positive voice. I realised - and this is going to sound more arrogant than I mean it to be - that people seem to gravitate towards me and I was never the right person to be in that position. Like, do you remember Danny's younger sisters?"

Vanessa nodded, hand over her mouth as she ate.

"Tilly would always listen to everything I said like it was the secret to life. And I look back at how I was, and the example I set, and feel awful. It's nice to think maybe I have a chance to do better now."

The girls paid, leaving a good tip, and caught the bus to the outer district, where they had to change. They decided to make the most of the pleasant evening, knowing they didn't have many warm ones left, and walked for forty minutes, admiring the city skyline, to Brooke's brother's house.

The roads were lit by the moon and streetlights when they arrived. Stef had already put Beau to bed, despite his protesting. Brooke and Vanessa were quiet as they sat in the living room where Ali had already set their sleeping arrangements.

Ali mentioned the time the girls stayed when they were younger.

"You'd come to watch a show or something?"

"Oh yeah. That was my fourteenth birthday!" Brooke began. "We'd convinced our parents to let us get the coach by ourselves for the first time."

"We got lost literally straight away," Vanessa added.

Ali joined. "And then you called me, and I was on a test drive with a client."

Brooke suppressed her laughter. "And your client drove through the city to pick us up and drop us at the theatre."

"She sat there trying to make small talk with you two while I was trying to give my sales pitch."

Vanessa and Brooke cringed.

"And she kept asking us what we thought. But she was just really weird about it … Did she buy it?" asked Vanessa.

"I think she did!"

The three struggled to contain their humour.

"Did you ever tell my parents?" Brooke asked.

"No, I think I just told them I picked you up and brought you both straight here. But they probably knew I was lying."

The girls took Beau to school the next morning before heading back. Brooke dropped Vanessa at The Cafe and she ran up to Blaine's to get changed into a uniform.

As Brooke pulled up in the drive, her dad came out the front door.

"Chuck the keys." His hands were already out ready to catch them. "I've got a lecture I'm covering this afternoon in the city."

Brooke tossed the keys in an arc through the air and they floated into his hands.

"I'll just grab my bags out the back quick. Why the sudden Friday afternoon lecture?"

"They've had a professor leave just as term started and apparently most of these students on the course keep asking for me so they suggested I come in again a little earlier for a chat."

"So does this mean a possible full-time position?"

"It could be. Would be nice to have something more permanent now; plus I'd be closer to my grandchildren now the second one is on its way. So we'll just wait and see what happens."

"Sounds good!" Brooke put the bags down and gave him a hug.

"I am so proud of you, BeeBee. You've made so much progress this year, and it is admirable."

"Where is this coming from?"

"Seeing you with this much structure and control lately. Your drive to get into the world is starting to turn you into the strong woman I knew you could be, but feared you wouldn't allow yourself to be. It's really good to finally see her take her rightful place."

Brooke's smile shook.

"Fuck off," she said in jest as they both began to laugh. "You're getting soft in your old age." Brooke gave him another hug, picked up her bags, and walked towards the front door.

"I hope it goes well today. I re-fuelled just outside of town so you'll be good to make it to Ali's for the evening."

He climbed into the driver's seat.

She chucked her bags inside the door, turned back, and called out to him.

"Dad!"

He looked over intently.

"Thank you for being patient with me."

The smile he returned was delicate.

"Patience, my lord?" he responded. "Why, it is the soul of peace. Of all the virtues 'tis nearest kin to heaven."

She sighed. It was the quote he had always used when she was growing up. Brooke shook her head and finished the last line for him.

"It makes men look like gods."

He shut the door and pulled off the drive.

The Brother

The chilled autumn air snuck through Blaine's window, waking both him and Vanessa. It seemed like the first time in ages they'd both spent the night together. She'd been busy with shoots and early shifts at The Cafe. He'd been busy with late night shifts at Kestrel.

Vanessa loved the convenience of a key to the apartment, being able to take the odd shower upstairs and leave Blaine little surprises to find when he got home. He never failed to pop down to The Cafe for lunchtime visits.

They cuddled in closer, wrapping the covers tighter, stealing each other's warmth. Trying to appreciate this calm moment, Vanessa groaned.

"I have to pee but I don't want to move."

"Just piss the bed," Blaine replied.

She laughed as she threw the covers off and shuffled to the bathroom. He watched, admiring her, before she disappeared, leaving the door ajar. Vanessa came back to bed and the two enjoyed each other's company.

Hours passed yet the moments felt eternal. They went from relaxing in bed, to watching Barbarella, followed by a stroll into town to pick up ingredients for dinner, returning home to cook a risotto, listening to the radio for once — Home by Adjust the Sails played.

"It's nice to hear good music making a comeback to the mainstream," they agreed.

Vanessa took her bowl out onto the roof and sat on the

floor with her back against the milk crate, watching the clouds caress the orange parts of the sky. Blaine handed Vanessa two glasses of water and climbed out, sitting on the other milk crate.

They ate, deep in thought, watching the sky.

"What's running through your head, Vans?"

"Life."

"Deep." Blaine moved down to the floor beside her. "Mind if I join?"

She shuffled up against him and rested her head on his shoulder.

They watched the clouds float. Blaine took the tip of Vanessa's chin and brought it his, kissing her on the lips.

"It's nice to enjoy the simple things."

Vanessa hummed. "Yeah, it's nice to just take a step back and rest."

Blaine pulled a blanket off the washing line and laid it across their legs. Vanessa kissed him on the cheek and rested her head back on his shoulder. Listening to the static of traffic as tree branches were moved in the breeze, they stayed outside a little longer until the sky rolled from orange to pink and back into a dark blue.

It felt as if they were the only two breathing the cool night air. Vanessa moved between his legs and his hands wrapped around her waist.

"I think I will enjoy winter this year," she said, pulling his wrists further around.

"Why, because you will be in a hot country?" he asked.

"Yeah, partly that, but also just have a hunch it'll be a good winter."

Blaine smiled as he kissed the crown of her head.

"Me too."

As the evening air began to chill, Vanessa and Blaine

climbed back inside and showered together, getting into bed for an early night. Vanessa fiddled with The Feather Necklace as it lay on his chest, before he took it off and hung it on the lamp.

The alarm sounded at 7:30 and Vanessa had to drag Blaine out of bed. Putting on their sweats, they left the house for Vanessa's morning jog, each listening to different music — Blaine, a collection of 90s hip-hop, and Vanessa to Sum 41.

The morning air was crisp and stung Blaine's face; Vanessa, in her element, enjoyed the breeze.

They looped back to the apartment and sat at the dining table, the latest addition of furniture, for breakfast. Vanessa smiled, looking around at this place that had become a second home to her, remembering how bare it used to be.

She blew on her tea. "I need to cut your hair again soon."

Blaine pulled a strand of his fringe down, looking at it, crossing his eyes.

"Yeah, it is due, I think."

"Tonight?"

"It's a date!"

He spooned his cereal.

Vanessa changed into her work clothes, Blaine distracting her to keep her in her underwear. She blushed at his compliments; his charm still caught her by surprise. Standing in the doorway, her hair up in a messy bun, two strands drifting down and framing her face, dimples glowing, Vanessa pecked him on the lips.

"Have a good day, my love," Blaine said, hand reached out to touch hers until the last moment.

"You too, Boo." Their fingertips sparked as they separated and Vanessa left.

~~~

A wet and dull autumn day. Blaine had been down to see Vanessa for breakfast. She looked exhausted after yet another modelling job for a pumpkin patch advertisement campaign the day before.

Blaine sat in the apartment, bored, leaving for work an hour early. He walked into Kestrel just after 3:00. Tim stood behind the bar with Brooke, neither looking very productive despite a few large tables.

"Yay, you're early. You can deal with these knobs," Brooke said, cotched against the beer fridge.

Tim was beside her. "It's some sort of bachelor-party-road-trip thing, just a bunch of rich white men."

"You're a rich white man," Blaine remarked.

Tim smirked. "Sorry … young, disrespectful, rich white men."

"Ah. I see."

Blaine and Brooke chuckled.

Going to the back to put his coat and bag away, Blaine heard a familiar voice talking to Brooke.

"What's a pretty little thing like you doing working in a shitty town like this?" The Man's voice dripped arrogance.

Brooke said nothing, poured his drink with a service smile, her eyes down.

"Oh, come on, I know you've got a prettier smile than that."

Blaine felt sick when he saw the face that matched the voice.

"Still not learned about charm yet then, Darren?" he said.

The Man's face dropped. Brooke's eyebrows scrunched.

"Fuck. Me. Look who's still kicking." Darren's voice, venomous, continued, "Never thought we'd see you again."

Brooke's face screwed up even more.

Blaine stayed silent, while Darren's voice soured the air.

"So this is where you ended up then, 'ey?"

Blaine nodded as he poured the other pint.

"Jimmy will be pissed he missed you. He's meeting us in the next town … It's my bachelor party!"

Blaine said nothing.

"I'll tell him you said hi?" Darren taunted.

"Sure."

Blaine placed the glass down and read out his total.

Darren paid and scoffed at him.

"Such a shame … It's a good thing Father can't see you right now. He'd be so disappointed."

Blaine held his tongue but Brooke could see his eyes burning. Darren walked back over to the group.

Brooke whispered, "Are you all good, B?"

"I was." He exhaled.

"So is that …"

"Drop it, Brooke."

Blaine went to the stockroom. Tim and Brooke shared an uncomfortable look and she followed Blaine.

"Brooke … Please, just go back."

She walked away. Blaine composed himself and came onto the floor, straight over to Tim.

He took a deep breath and, in a low voice, said, "I need to leave."

"Okay."

"It's just if I stay, I know I'll …"

"Blaine, it's okay. I'll give Amanda a call. You don't need to explain anything to me." Tim placed his hand on Blaine's shoulder.

"Thank you." Blaine struggled to keep his composure as he walked over to the bar, and took Brooke's hand.

"Sorry I snapped at you."

"I love you, B. Just want you to be okay, okay?"

"Careful, girly!" Darren shouted from across the bar. "Don't get too close. Pretty girls tend to die around that one."

The sound of a glass smashing against the edge of the table beside him shattered Darren's laugh. Brooke tensed. She looked up to see Blaine's face burning with rage.

"There he is! There's the Blaine I know!" Darren cheered.

Blaine stormed around the bar but Tim stepped into his path.

"B ... Leave now," he whispered into his ear, blocking him.

Blaine froze, seeing Brooke watch him in terror.

"I am so sorry," Blaine said to Tim. His eyes red but tearless, he walked towards the door.

"Running away as usual, Brother? Fucking disgrace to the family, mate!" Darren shouted across the bar.

Blaine stopped and turned to face Darren.

"Me? The Disgrace? I think that's a matter of perspective. And, you are not my family. The people in this town are my family, and up until this moment I had never disgraced them. All I've done is honour anyone I've loved. Honour! Something you'll never know. "

Tim glared at Blaine.

"Send your new wife my commiserations." Blaine walked out of the bar and down the street, away from his brother.

His phone buzzed in his pocket but he ignored it. The buzz in his mind was louder. Blaine's thoughts were flooded with memories of his past. Of growing up, of university, of his father and his mother ... of Yalena.

Red-faced and broken-hearted, he burst out crying as he paced through the streets towards his home. Pulling his hoodie up to hide his face, he took a different turn to make sure he didn't walk past The Cafe window.

Blaine ran into his room, grabbed his travelling bag, and started ramming clothes inside. Each time he tried to clear his head, it went back to his brother's voice and his anger returned. Slamming cupboards, Blaine frantically looked, unsure of what he was looking for.

A sign, anything, something to tell me what to do.

Something smashed against the floor. He saw a handle and pieces of ceramic shattered across the kitchen. He had knocked The Mug from the counter.

There it is ... there is your sign, he thought as he bent down to pick up one of the shards, cutting the tip of his finger. *It was fun while it lasted ... but nothing good lasts ... how stupid are you that you actually started to believe this could last?*

Blaine walked back over to his bag, stuffing his old hoodie in when he heard a voice.

"Do I not even get a goodbye kiss?"

Through blurred eyes he saw Vanessa in the doorway. She glanced at his bloody hand clenching the piece, cutting into his palm.

Blaine said nothing. He stood, paralyzed.

Vanessa walked into the kitchen, grabbed a cloth, and slowly walked to his side. She raised his forearm and opened up his fist. Removing the broken piece, she wrapped his hand with the cloth.

"He's right," Blaine muttered as Vanessa continued to wrap his hand. "I am a disgrace. Look at how quickly I've fucked everything up. I ruin everything."

"You've ruined nothing, Blaine." Vanessa kissed his cheek.

"I had finally escaped it all. But it still found me ... of course it did."

"So what? You just pack up and run? It will find you again, so why run?"

"So I don't hurt the people I love."

Vanessa held his hand.

"You know how dumb that logic is, right?" Blaine looked up from the floor. "You leaving would hurt us so much more."

He gasped, choking on each words, until one finally got out.

"Home."

A tear rolled down Vanessa's cheek.

"Home is more than a mug." He sputtered a laugh through his tears. "Home is where your heart loves because it is safe. Family are the people who love you."

"Is this your home?"

Blaine nodded. "I have found my family."

She pulled him into her arms.

"I love you, Vanessa Gretchen."

Vanessa explained how Brooke messaged her, worried when he wouldn't answer. Tim and Brooke listened to Darren spit bile about Blaine. Neither absorbed any of it. They knew who Blaine was and this ghost from his past wouldn't change that. Darren was told to leave Kestrel immediately.

Vanessa spent the evening listening to Blaine talk about his past.

"Yalena was the one who persuaded me to get away from my family. She said 'blood loses its strength if it's infected.' Brooke's face, the way she looked at me, was exactly how Yalena would look when I'd been around my family."

They watched *Casablanca* and ordered in Chinese.

Blaine eventually fell asleep in Vanessa's arms. She watched him, his mind finally at peace, as were the pieces from his past.

The next few days he walked the streets as prying eyes watched him like The Outsider. Tim reassured him everything was okay.

"To be honest, it was good to see that side of you. I never trust someone who is always decent … feels like they are hiding something. I think most people are just a little disappointed that their original theories are wrong."

"Sorry for the broken glass."

"No need to apologise, mate. I'm more pissed that you missed."

Brooke took Blaine over to Wayton, him in the back seat instead this time, his music playing in her father's Jeep — Blink-182.

Blaine opened up to her about Yalena.

"I'm sorry it's taken me this long to tell you about her. And I feel like a dick for the way I acted that day."

"Dude, honestly, it's fine. I was a little turned on." She parked in a quiet neighbourhood. "It explains why you have so much wisdom, though. Sounds like you've had a very intense past."

Blaine grimaced. "It's been a lot, and I think I've only just processed it all."

"Well, you have us now. An outside voice always helps to broaden your perspective. You've taught me that."

Excitement faded and the story of The Bartender throwing a glass became no more than an inside joke at Kestrel. Autumn was in full swing, the rain testament to that.

Blaine was working a quiet lunch shift, the bar empty. He spent the majority of time watching the car lights dance through the rain droplets on the window. A young man walked in and smiled over at him, reserved and nervous. Blaine didn't know whether to laugh or run in fear.

"I come in peace," The Guy said.

"Hi, Jimmy."

"Hey, big brother, Darren told me I might find you here."

"What do you want, Jimmy?"

"To see how you're doing."

Jimmy walked over and sat at the bar.

"I was doing perfectly fine until the past walked through that door," Blaine said, tipping his head towards the entrance.

"Well, after it walks out you'll go back to that. I promise."

Blaine scoffed at his brother's words but said nothing. Jimmy shuffled in his chair.

"The family fell apart after you left. She left Dad in the end. Darren got into some shady business and Dad started drinking again."

"And that's my fault, is it?"

"Darren and Dad think so ... But no, it's not. You were just the catalyst. It's been a mess our whole lives. It was bound to happen eventually."

There was a pause before Blaine asked, "How is she?"

He picked up a glass to offer Jimmy a drink. Jimmy declined.

"Not sure. She did a you and vanished. The night before, she told me she was proud of you for escaping Dad's grip and hoped someday I'd do the same."

"Have you?"

Jimmy gave a half smile. "I graduated a few months ago and have been offered a position to teach abroad."

Blaine blinked. "Congratulations, Jimmy. Life is working out for you."

"Yeah, I guess. Should thank you for that. The last night you were home opened my eyes and having her leave was a wake-up call. Made me notice how toxic things had been and I was just ignorant to it all."

The bar was silent as the rain hit the glass.

"So … how are you?" Jimmy asked.

"Happy."

He relaxed into his chair. "Good! Sorry, I know you don't want anything to do with us anymore, but after Darren told me you were here, I had to see you." Jimmy's eyes twinkled at his older brother. "You look good! Happiness suits you, Blaine."

Blaine shook his head as a smile broke through. "I'm glad you woke up. I was so worried you'd end up like them."

"You were The Brother who inspired me, even when we were young. Smart and strong-willed. You always did what was right even if you knew Dad would punish you for it."

"That's why I left."

Jimmy looked at his watch. "Well, I guess I'd best be leaving, too."

Blaine looked up at his brother as he stood.

Jimmy held out his hand. "It's good to see you smile. Have a happy life, Brother."

Blaine shook Jimmy's hand across the bar.

"And you, Jim." A smile remained on Blaine's face.

"And don't worry. I'll tell them I came here and found out you'd skipped town. No one will disturb your peace anymore."

Blaine nodded back.

As Jimmy left, Brooke walked in for her shift.

"Who's that?" she asked.

Blaine took a deep breath.

"Closure."

The Fresh Start

Autumn passed. Fallen leaves lay golden. October rolled into November. Vanessa worked at The Cafe, taking a step away from the modelling until her big job. Brooke spent more time in the city and less time working in Kestrel, the new fashion line launching in a few weeks.

Blaine was beginning to feel the Christmas spirit: the cold crisp days, multiple layers of clothes, Vanessa getting him into winter fashion with scarves, beanies and toques. He said he wanted to put the tree up and decorate before Vanessa left for Bali but she argued that it would be too early.

Brooke drove home from the city late one evening, missing her own bed. The drive felt effortless, as she listened to early 00s and late 90s music.

I've been hanging out with Blaine and Vanessa for too long, she chuckled to herself after singing the words to Blink-182 — San Diego.

Guided by street lights, she admired the contrast between the artificial light and the moonlight.

She passed the "Welcome To Town" sign sooner than expected, the car parked itself on the drive, her key was in the door, and her feet floated up the stairs. Brooke collapsed onto her bed, kicking off her shoes, shuffling out of her skirt, then wandering to her bathroom in her bra, brushing her teeth, wiping away her make-up, and washing away the drawn-on beauty mark.

The late morning sun poked through the blinds but did not wake her. Her phone buzzing did. She smiled as she stretched, well-rested.

> 11:29 - missed call from Vanessa
>
> 11:16 - Vanessa: Winter market this evening are you still down?
>
> 9:22 - Blaine: spend the day with us??? Demi is coming for the market later so figured we'd grab lunch and do something until then considering we actually all have the same day off for once.
>
> 9:22 - Blaine: make the most of it.

Brooke unlocked her phone and called Vanessa.

"Hey," Brooke morning-voiced.

"Morning sleepy head," Vanessa crackled through the speaker. "We are at Kestrel, Tim called Blaine. It's busy in here."

"Not surprised."

"Yeah, me neither. I'm sat at the bar with a glass of mulled wine. Let me know when you are on your way and I'll get Blaine to pour you a glass."

"Okay, no dramas, I'll be there soon, Boo."

"Bye-bye BeeBee."

"Byee."

Brooke put on a pair of thick leggings, a vest-top, turtleneck jumper, and her winter coat. Downstairs, her mother made her a coffee. The walk was brisk, cold winter air sharp on her face, the coffee warm in her hands. When she got to Kestrel, Blaine and Mel were both behind the bar making winter-themed cocktails, the aroma of mulled cider and wine filling the bar.

Vanessa and Brooke sat for the next hour enjoying a bottle of Malbec as the bar quietened down and Blaine clocked out. The three of them left to meet Demi at the bus station and strolled to the market.

Stalls were threaded with lights waiting for sunset. Spices filled the air as they walked from booth to booth, choosing free samples of hot foods and drinks to warm cold hands, checking out the knick-knacks and Christmas decorations asking to be homed.

Vanessa fell in love with a fluffy snowman the size of her head, so Blaine bought it for her and said it could live at his place. She named it Jenifer. Blaine picked up some tinsel and lights for the apartment.

"I am genuinely so excited to decorate this year!" he said. "The last time I was excited for Christmas and actually celebrated I must have been like twelve? So I'm going all out!"

Brooke and Demi giggled at him as he wore a dancing hat with elf ears and walked, unfazed and cheerful, through the crowd.

Blaine and Vanessa wandered up to pick out a tree, leaving Brooke and Demi to sit and eat their steaming pasties.

"How's the new line coming?" Demi asked.

"Honestly, I need to thank you! It is such a great opportunity. It's going so well but it's exhausting going back and forth from here every week."

"Why don't you move there?"

"I stay with my brother but I wouldn't want to be living with him full-time."

"Get your own place?"

Brooke's pasty dripped on the ground. "I can't afford that yet! Plus I wouldn't want to live alone, I'd get lonely."

"You know me." Demi gave her a cheeky smile. "And you'd meet people."

Brooke paused and gave a slow, considerate nod.

"I was thinking of moving into a new place. We could do it together."

Brooke's eyes widened. "Really? ... That would be kind of cool."

"Yeah. We get on, it'll be a laugh."

"Okay. Sure. Yeah, let's do it!"

"Sweet. Whenever you're next in the city, hit me up and we'll go for lunch and talk about it more."

The next morning Blaine popped down to see Vanessa, as usual, and sat at the table by the window. Vanessa watered the hanging plants, sat with him, then took his order to the kitchen. Dean came out.

"Good morning, Blaine." Dean walked over to the table.

"Morning!"

"I handed Mick my notice a couple days ago."

"You're leaving? Why?"

"You."

"Me? What did I do?"

Dean sat opposite him in the booth. "You've inspired me and the boyfriend. We've both wanted to travel for years but blamed being in our thirties as an excuse. Watching you, here, now settled after coming on a whim ... we both thought, maybe we can do the same somewhere."

"Exciting stuff, man! I have to admit I do still get an itch to pack up every now and then."

"Yeah, figured I'm due a change of scenery."

"Where are you two going?" Blaine asked.

"Not sure yet, we are thinking of just buying a van and driving."

"In the winter?"

"No no," Dean chuckled, "We are going to his sister's for Christmas and then we'll go somewhere warm as a little holiday and do it in February. So I'm working out a month's notice, then the week Vanessa gets back from Bali, I'm off."

"Fair enough."

"So I just wanted to thank you for the inspiration."

"Anything to help people live their best life."

"Right, I should get back in that kitchen and sort out your breakfast," Dean said, placing his hands on the table and pushing himself to his feet.

Vanessa's flight to Bali was three days away. She realised she had not been overthinking every possible outcome, and was at the mercy of fate. This idea no longer frightened her.

She caved and agreed to let Blaine put the decorations up. The smile on his face convinced her.

They spent the day snacking, laughing, dancing, and listening to cheesy Christmas music — including country Christmas songs. Baubles hung, lights wrapped around the tree, and tinsel lay about the apartment. As she spun around under the tinsel they had pinned to the ceiling, Vanessa's dimples mesmerised Blaine.

She leapt into his arms for a hug after catching him smiling at her. He squeezed her tighter than usual, bringing his face into the base of her neck. He kissed her neck and then her shoulder, noticing her perfume. Blaine smiled into her neck and inhaled, repeatedly kissing her.

Vanessa felt him squeeze tighter.

"B?"

"I'm going to miss you more than I think I've let myself process."

"Blaine ..." Vanessa felt a lump in her throat.

He grabbed her hand, an excited look on his face.

"Let's go to The Basketball Court for sunset. Like right now."

Vanessa gave a timid nod.

They walked down in warm coats and sat, silent, watching the sky, hand in hand.

"I am going to miss you, too. So much."

Blaine let go of her hand and took The Feather Necklace from around his neck, putting it around Vanessa's.

"This was Yalena's," he said, the pendant resting in the palm of his hand.

"Her father gave it to her before she went to Uni. She was nervous about leaving home even though travelling was her life. It was more the leaving her family."

Vanessa spun it around in her fingers as it hung around her neck.

"He said it was to remind her to be light-hearted and kind even when life made it hard. He said for it to remind her not to forget how strong she is and to always let the beauty of her soul guide her."

"Blaine ... I. I can't ..."

"He gave it to me at her funeral and told me the same thing. He said not to forget to look for beauty and love even when the world looks dark." Blaine choked up. "This has been a big part of me and whenever I look at it, I am reminded of her smile when I need it most."

"B ..."

"I have you now, Vanessa." Blaine took a step back to witness Vanessa model the necklace. "And seeing you with a part of her makes me so happy. I've found my beauty and love again."

Vanessa buried her head into his chest.

"I love you so much, Blaine," she whispered.

"Besides," he said as he wiped a tear from his eye, "she always wanted to go to Bali and I promised I'd take her. This is my way of keeping that promise."

Vanessa chuckled, her cheeks wet and cold, and she kissed him.

The orange glow of the sky filled the court with a warm light and they sat a while longer before heading back to Blaine's for dinner.

~~~

And this, my dearest reader, is the point I'd like to leave our characters to go off on their own. As the New Year came, Brooke moved in with Demi and began her next chapter. The fashion line was a hit, and opportunities opened for Our Girl. Vanessa's photo shoot in Bali was a hit, and drew her even more from her shell.

Blaine continued at Kestrel, content with life's routine. Vanessa moved in with him at the beginning of February. The annoyances in each other became parts to love.

Vanessa, Demi, and Brooke secured a job together in the summer, posing on beaches in exotic lands. Blaine flew out to join them, planning a road trip through the jungle.

Dean and his boyfriend travelled. Mick and Jenny got pregnant with their second child. Amanda and Tim, having found company in each other at the Christmas party, grew closer. Brooke's father took a full-time position at the university, and became a big part of his son, his grandson, and his granddaughter's lives.

And the stories all continued.

Don't think this is me saying, "And they all lived happily ever after!" because it's not over yet. I've still got a little more to show you before you turn the last pages. I would just like to give them some privacy for the next part of their own stories.

The Man and The Woman

The Man sat at the bar, cold drink in hand, replaying the past ten years, pondering his youth. He had worked hard, far from any home.

He'd worked hard, but for what?

The Man took a sip.

The Woman entered, turning heads as usual. Except his. She sat with her friends at a table, glancing over to him, her eyes drawn to him. She could not see his face but his presence comforted her.

The ladies giggled and laughed, flirting.

The Woman approached the bar and ordered a fruit cider. Her voice flowed through his ears like an old melody.

He turned to look. Their eyes met.

"Danny?"

"Hey, Katie!"

Katie moved closer. "Hi! What are the chances?"

"I know! How long has it been? Eight years?"

"It must be. How are you?" Katie wrapped her arms around him.

She took him over to her table and introduced him, then said goodbye to the girls. "See you back at the hotel."

Danny and Katie strolled the late evening streets, Danny tall and handsome, Katie in a black pencil dress with knee-high boots. Arms linked, they reminisced.

"I miss those days."

"Drinking with no worry of a hangover!"

"And the freedom!"

The live blues from a jazz bar welcomed them in. Sitting in a candlelit booth, they ordered a bottle of Rioja.

"I still can't get over the fact I bumped into you."

"Serendipity," Danny said, raising his glass.

"A beautiful turn of fate." She touched her glass to his. "So what are you doing in this part of the world?"

"I'm here for a job interview. But I'm not sure if I want to take it."

"How come?"

"I like my current job. It's just not taking me anywhere in life, ya know."

"Yeah, I get you. The routine is growing old. It's a constant loop I just can't escape."

"Literally."

"I think that's just your late twenties, though?" Katie frowned. "Like what, I'm twenty-eight nearly twenty-nine, you're ...?"

"Thirty."

"Ouch."

Danny scoffed. "Tell me about it. I feel like I've wasted my life."

Katie sat with her chin in her hands.

Danny took a sip of the wine, topping both glasses. "Like, I finished Uni and struggled to get a job position higher than a glorified coffee boy. Meanwhile, there was Brooke becoming semi-famous as a fashion icon. It made me question if I was doing it right."

"I don't think there is a 'right way' anymore, if I'm being honest. I think you exist to just exist. You do you and just try to be happy."

They both sat. Katie's eyes wandered to the band.

Danny tapped his glass with his ring. "Are you happy, Katie?"

"I was. I was very happy for a long time. But those things that used to bring me happiness no longer do."

"Maybe that's a good thing, though." Danny shrugged. "Like, do you remember that summer we both fell out with Brooke?"

"The one where you guys broke up to go to Uni? Or, the one where she became a selfish bitch and thought she was better than us?"

Danny chuckled. "The last time I think we all saw each other."

Katie pursed her lips. "Sooo, the time she thought she was better than us."

Danny shook his head, smiling. "I think I finally understand why that happened and she became so distant with us."

Katie leaned in, feigning intrigue.

"Her interests in life changed and we grew apart … and I think that's how I feel with my job. It's such a contradiction, because I do still love it and it's safe but I just don't feel right anymore. It's hard to explain."

"No, I think I get what you mean. It's that gut feeling."

"Yeah! And it's so hard to fight."

Now serious, she took his hand. "Then don't. Listen to it. Trust your instincts. You're smarter than you give yourself credit for, Danny. Always have been."

Katie blushed and turned her head away. Danny's mind cleared.

"You're right. Change is coming, I need to embrace it."

They ordered another bottle of wine, returning to the world around them.

Outside, under streetlights, a warm breeze caressed the street.

"It's not too far to my hotel. If you fancy the walk?" Katie asked.

"Of course."

The Man and The Woman strolled through the city, shoulder to shoulder. Danny walked Katie up to her room.

"This was really nice," Katie whispered, looking up at him.

"It was," he whispered back. "Thank you for the company this evening. It's been good to catch up."

"We've always gotten each other."

Katie stood in the doorway, smiling at the floor. As she peered up, Danny stepped closer.

"We should grab lunch," he suggested. "Tomorrow, before you leave?"

"I'd like that. There is a lovely place on Cork Street. Meet me by the clock tower at 11:30."

"It's a date." Danny kissed her on the cheek. "Goodnight, Katharine."

"Goodnight, Dan." She peered around the closing door. "See you in the morning."

Danny waited until the door clicked then walked back under the yellow lights of the city.

~~~

Katie stood under the clock tower, suitcase by her side, bag on her shoulder, and bottle of water in hand. Danny walked over, took her suitcase, and wheeled it down to the restaurant, sitting outside on a picnic table.

"So, I'm taking your Courtesan phase is behind you?"

Katie laughed and kicked him under the table. "I guess you could say that ... But in a way it's still kind of who I am. I don't sleep around anymore ... as much. I crave intimacy more now. Talking with someone, the closeness. Lying there, listening to the deep breathing after. Cooking breakfast, or running to grab food to get more energy."

"I swear it was mainly couscous."

"Because couscous is perfect!"

They shared a laugh.

"But no," Katie continued. "Yeah, people would always try to shame me for it, but I don't regret anything. I learned exactly what I'm looking for when it comes to a man and a relationship from those experiences, and they also taught me a lot about myself, too."

She sat up straight in her chair and finished the rest of her sentence properly enunciating each word as if it was the conclusion in an essay.

"However, I guess you could say the courtesan lifestyle no longer satisfies me like it used to. I'm looking for something a little more long-term now."

"Yeah, I get that. I dated someone for just over three years and I broke up with her last year because it just felt like there was something missing. It wasn't the relationship I wanted for the rest of my life."

Katie winced and groaned, "It's hard, right! Such high expectations but so pressured to get it right straight away."

"Guess it really is right place, right time."

They both looked down at the table, deep in thought. Their legs brushed and brought attention back to the other.

"I'm not worried, though. I trust my instincts."

"Good!"

"I've stopped trying to be someone I'm not in order to please the people around me. Acting that way made me a lost person after University."

"So how is living for you working out?" she asked as if conducting an interview, Danny played along, giving a look of consideration to his answer, weighing the pros and cons.

"My circle is definitely a lot smaller. I don't speak to a lot of people that much anymore. But the right ones always seem to stay."

"Are you happier?"

He nodded. "I'm definitely getting there."

Danny asked for the cheque, Katie insisting on paying.

"How about I get this one, and you come to visit me at some point and take me out for dinner?" she said, putting her card in the machine.

He smiled at her confidence; he'd missed it.

"Sounds like a fair deal to me. But only if we plan the date here and now?" Danny looked through the calendar on his phone, considering next month but his mouth spoke for him instead. "Two weeks from now?"

"It's a date! Something to get me through the day-to-day shit when I get back."

Danny threw his bag on his back, taking Katie's suitcase once more, and walked her to the bus station. As they went inside, Katie took her suitcase off him and moved a strand of hair from her face.

They hugged goodbye and Katie kissed his lips, both pulling away slow, eyes closed, and Katie's hand pressed against his chest. The kiss was sweet and brief, neither leaning in for a second. Smiling as they stood eyes locked, Katie giggled, shaking her head and collecting her thoughts.

"I'll text you my address when I get on the bus. It was really good to see you, Danny."

"Have a safe journey back, and I will see you soon," he said, taking his hands off of her hips.

"You too, see you very soon!"

Katie smiled at the floor. *I've missed you,* she thought as she walked away.

She'd only taken a few steps into the queue when he called out to her. She turned back to see his smile beam through the station.

"I've missed you!"

The old lady behind her let out a sigh of admiration at the scene.

Katie's scarlet lips formed with confidence and replied, "Then don't wait two weeks, kay?"

Pulling out her phone, she typed something then put it back in her pocket.

Danny's phone buzzed.

"Now you know where to find me." She called back across the station. "See you soon!"

They stood smiling at each other across the platform before she giggled, blowing him a kiss, and walked away to get on her bus.

See you soon.

The Outsider

A beautiful spring day, the first of many after a long, wet winter. Our Outsider stood alone in their new apartment — Blink-182, Miss You, playing through headphones. The spring sun warmed the room.

The Outsider stood, grateful. How different everything is now. *Time for the next journey.*

Staring into an apartment with nothing but a sofa and a bed in the next room, she began to unpack before wandering around this new town. As late afternoon approached, the bed made up and pictures hung on the walls with pride, The Outsider left the apartment, wandering the streets with a signature smile.

She found a noodle place, ordered sweet and sour chicken, and sat on a bench by The Lake to watch the last of the sunlight on the ripples.

It's so peaceful here, I could definitely get used to this.

A few days passed and Our Outsider settled into this new home, becoming friends with the neighbours and finding secret spots around town and by The Lake.

There was a knock at the door just before noon. The Outsider, knowing exactly who it was from the knock, ran to let them in. The door opened wide to a beautiful face, dimples framed by blonde strands of hair, arms open, revealing a pregnant belly.

"Look at you! You look stunning!" Our Outsider said.

"As do you! Come here and give me a hug, Beebee!"

Brooke pulled Vanessa in for a hug.

"Where are your bags?" Brooke asked.

"Blaine's just parking down the street and he'll bring them up, but I've been waiting nearly a year to see you, I couldn't wait another second!"

The girls sat in Brooke's sparse living room, jug of water out on the coffee table with three glasses. There was another knock on the door and Brooke leaped onto Blaine. He stumbled, dropping the bags as he caught her.

"Jeez, calm down!" he chuckled.

"No! Because you gonna have a Bubba!"

Blaine whispered, "I know! And I'm also going to have a wife!" Brooke went to scream but he cupped her mouth. "But that stays between me and you for a couple days, okay?"

Brooke nodded and he let go.

Blaine brought the bags in and sat down next to Vanessa. "So, Brooke, how was travelling around Southeast Asia and working out in Japan?" he asked.

"It was amazing! But I'm so glad to be settling down for a bit, I need a routine again."

"Modelling in Japan ... Must have been amazing!" Vanessa said.

"Do you miss it, V?"

"I do miss travelling to cool places for shoots but like you said, it's nice to have a routine, especially now. I'm doing a few pregnancy product campaigns so that'll be something a bit different."

"What are your plans, Brooke?" Blaine asked.

"I'm not really sure. I'm considering just getting a bartending job somewhere, or something. And I've been looking at summer University courses, to study psychology. I feel so privileged to have stumbled on these experiences so would like to help others who are lost."

"A mature student," Blaine contemplated. "It's never too late to get back into education."

"So what about you, mister? Are you still at Kestrel?"

"Of course," Blaine sighed. "Good pay, good tips, and I know the job like the back of my hand. However ..."

"Ooo! However what?"

Vanessa and Blaine looked at each other.

"Well, with a baby on the way we can't stay in the apartment, and the late hours aren't ideal anymore."

"Of course, of course." Brooke nodded.

"Tim is looking at branching out. So, he suggested that Kestrel go back into his management and I open up a bar-slash-restaurant down by the coast. Slow pace, live music, I'd manage and work days, and then hire a supervisor for evenings."

"That's awesome!"

"I know!" Vanessa squeaked. "We have been looking at houses by the coast and they are all so beautiful. Plus, the idea of live music! We've already talked about how nice it would be to get new, young, local bands involved."

"Aww, look at you two! All grown up and adult-y," Brooke said, scrunching up her face.

"Can you believe it was eight years ago this mysterious outsider showed up. And now, here I am, pregnant with his child," Vanessa joked.

"It's weird how life works out. And if you think about it, I'm The Outsider now."

"Don't worry it won't be for long." Blaine smiled.

Brooke noticed him peek over at Vanessa's bump then up at her dimples. "You two are going to be such amazing parents."

Vanessa took Blaine's hand and Brooke asked, "Have you thought of names yet?"

"We want to wait until the baby is born to find out the gender, but we are thinking Jack or Manni if it's a boy," Vanessa said. "And if it's a girl, Yalena."

"The perfect name for your offspring indeed."

Blaine chuckled. "Offspring?"

"I'm trying not to cry here, okay! Jeez!"

"So I properly should tell you we've also decided the last name will be Gretchen then?" Blaine teased.

A tear brushed Brooke's cheek. "That's so beautiful!"

"Yalena Brooke Gretchen? It sort of works?" he continued.

"Oh, fuck off!" Brooke hugged them both. "You better call her that now if it's a girl!"

Blaine held the girls tight. "I found my true family with Vans, so it only seemed right for us to use her name."

Vanessa pulled The Feather Necklace from her top. "When we were at the beach last month, a man saw me wearing this, and asked where I had gotten it, just as Blaine came over. It was Yalena's father."

"Woah ..."

"You should hear some of the stories from when Blaine and Yalena travelled. Honestly, I don't understand how he has never been arrested!

"Honestly ... same," Blaine said. "Vanessa suggested the idea to them and Yalena's parents approved."

"It is a wonderful idea. I love it!" Brooke said. "What are the chances of bumping into them? Right place, right time, I guess."

Vanessa shrugged. "Like you said, everything finds its way."

The three went out for a meal that evening. Vanessa craved Indian, so Indian it was. They all made an effort to look nice and agreed tomorrow evening they'd just cook and lounge instead, watching a film with some snacks.

Brooke had bought a sofa bed but failed to assemble it

so she and Vanessa shared the bed the first night and Blaine took the blow-up mattress he had brought, just in case.

Vanessa was still asleep when they woke, so Blaine and Brooke went to the market to buy breakfast. The lakeside town was a dream for Brooke, with the prettiest sunsets. It was a communal town. The market had local products from nearby farms, and stores were small businesses run by residents at fair prices.

They picked up fresh bread and cheese from The Bakery, sausages and bacon in The Butchers, as well as fruit at The Grocers.

"I'm trying to be healthy at the moment," Brooke explained. "I'm cutting out most meats and experimenting with smoothies and shakes."

"One of the farms I worked at, The Farmer used to make the best smoothie: blueberry, strawberry, mango, honey, yoghurt, milk, turmeric. I owe so many hung-over morning recoveries to them."

"Let's do it. Not the hangover part, though."

They walked back the long way, past The Lake.

"I can't believe you are only just about to ask Vanessa to marry you," Brooke said, peering over the paper bag she was cradling, both hands on the bottom.

"There was never any rush. We both love each other and have known for the longest time that we will spend the rest of our lives together. Now she's pregnant, the time is right."

"See, you're such a spontaneous person, but so go with the flow at the same time. I thought you would have done it ages ago?"

"I nearly did it that first Christmas." They walked down the path that ran alongside the lake, the morning sun bouncing off the water. "But I knew how intense that would have been. I mean we moved in together pretty quick, but still. Vans mellowed me so much after Yalena. I was so scared that the next moment could be ripped away at any second, but Vanessa taught me to relax and not put pressure on things."

"And I think you taught her to take leaps of faith. She would have just settled with things at surface level."

Blaine smiled. "Yeah. We are good for each other."

"You really are! You balance each other out, which is why I am so jealous of that kid. Seriously, you two are going to be such good parents."

"And you are going to be such a great cool aunt!" Blaine gave her little nudge.

"Well, I have had the practice."

They arrived back at Brooke's place, Vanessa now awake, and they cooked breakfast.

Blaine assembled the sofa bed with Brooke, providing Vanessa with entertainment. They set it up for the evening and walked down to sit by The Lake. Dog walkers passed each other and chatted, young teen couples soaked in the sun, and a mother tried to keep control of her kids as they chased the ducks.

"It's a really nice place you've found here, BeeBee," Vanessa said, lying back on the picnic blanket.

"Yeah. I've missed this, though. Being with you two."

"We'll let you know once we are all moved into a new place, and our door will always be open. I know it will be more than a four-hour drive from here so we'll always have a place for you to sleep over. Bubba is going to need Auntie Brooke to lead her astray," Blaine said as Vanessa gently kicked him and Brooke belly laughed.

Brooke rolled over to rest her head on Vanessa's thigh.

"I will definitely be taking up that offer a lot. I miss you guys so much."

"We miss you too, Brooke. It's quiet in that town without you." Vanessa stroked Brooke's hair.

The spring breeze was cold. Blaine put his jacket around Vanessa.

"I bet. I forgot to ask what the latest gossip is?"

Blaine and Vanessa laughed, shaking their heads.

"You're worse than my mother, I swear," Vanessa said. "Nothing much really. You know about Mick's affair, right?"

"No!" Brooke sat up.

Blaine tutted. "We shouldn't get involved, Vans."

"Uh, yes we should! I worked for that man for years. I watched him treat that wonderful woman like nothing more than a housewife and squash her. I say she is better off without him. I just feel so bad for poor Sam and Billy. Billy is only seven so he doesn't really understand it all but Sam is nearly eleven."

"Now who's worse than your mother?" Blaine teased.

Vanessa took a deep breath. "Sorry ... hormones. It just makes me sick. I grew up working for him thinking he was such a great guy but I look back and he's always been such a dick!"

"So what happened?" Brooke asked.

"He hired a waitress just before the Christmas period," Blaine explained. "Started working later and more shifts. People noticed and started to talk. Next thing we hear Jenny has taken the kids to her parents for a few weeks in the New Year. I spoke to her when she came back and she explained how much she gave up for him. Guess it's never too late to say, enough."

"Now who's worse than my mother?" Vanessa glared at him.

"Touché." Blaine and Brooke chuckled. "Hey, we all have our opinions and views. Does not mean we are right, though."

Brooke frowned. "Poor Jenny ..."

The sun began to set behind the trees.

"Should we head back to mine and grab some snacks for movie night?"

As they got to their feet, Blaine looked out over the lake and smiled to himself.

"Hey Vans, can you grab something out my top jacket pocket?"

"Of course B, what am I looking for ..."

Vanessa pulled out a ring box.

Blaine took the box out of her hand.

Vanessa's voice was soft. "Oh you little shit ... don't!"

Blaine went to drop down to one knee but Vanessa grabbed his wrist. Her dimples caught a tear. She whispered, "No, please. Don't kneel. Just hold my hand, please."

"Okay," Blaine mouthed.

"I love you, Vanessa. Each time I see you smile I'm reminded of seeing you beside me, in the mirror, after you first cut my hair, and I fall in love with our story all over again. So as we are about to start our family, I'd like to ask: Vanessa, will you do me the honour of letting me take your name and become Blaine Gretchen?"

Vanessa's bottom lip quivered as she nodded and squeezed his hand. Blaine took the ring from the box and placed it on her finger.

"Will You Marry Me?"

"Of Course!"

She grabbed hold of his face and kissed him.

"I love you so much, Blaine. Of course I will!"

And so, this lake is the place I would like to end for one main reason.

This Story is no longer just My Story.

It has become Our Story.

What is it about, to you?

What is it About (To Me)

This book has been cathartic. It started at a point in my life where I was lost and idle. The "plans" that I had became unachievable. I was waiting on a distant future that wasn't going to arrive. So I had to figure out what came next instead.

And thus The Book was born.

The title, ironically, started as a joke. When I told people I was writing a book, they would ask, "What is it about?" And I would reply with, "Yeah"... because I think I am funny ... But I realised that *that* was what it was about. It became a manifestation. A journey of self-discovery that cannot be taught, only learned.

When I began, a theme of prejudice and stereotypes became apparent: the idea of ""judging a book by its cover" - a person by their title. Fascinated by the psychology behind this, I wanted to see what happens when you allow a reader, if they wished, to challenge their own views on life and explore where they have come from - To ask not just what, but why. This is the reason for the characters' titles evolving as they grow in the story. It is also why personality, appearance, sexuality, and gender are revealed in a range of ways. For instance: What gender is the Mayor to you? Did you think The Outsider was male straight away? What ethnicity do you see in different characters?

Some of the answers are relative - simultaneously right and wrong.

During editing, Trevor made a comment that stuck with

me. He used the word "sketch" to describe the book. And I found that wonderful. I provided the outline, My World, but you built Our World according to the views of Your World.

I have a terrible habit (or wonderful personality trait, depending who you ask) of living as a phoenix, of building something from the ashes of the old. Writing this book has been no different. From the ashes of an old story, I started down a new path.

I hope you have taken something new away from this familiar story.

Thank you for joining me on this journey and hope you'll stick around for another, because there is plenty more where this came from.

Until next time

Finished on The Basketball Court where I came to think during spring of the 2020 pandemic, The place this story was conceived.

About The Author

Owen Crawford was born and raised in the south of England. Having spent his teen years curious about the worlds beyond his own, he entered his third decade wandering the opposite side of the planet. Fascinated by psychology, he now endeavours to explore further, not only the outside world, but also the inside world.

What is it About? is the first book of a hopeful career.

Follow the travels and inspirations of the next stories:
Instagram - @owencrawford_official
Website - www.poeticironypublishing.com
Facebook - @Poetic.Irony.Publishing